Mountain Mermen

The Complete Series

Kat Vroman

Copyright © 2024 by Kat Vroman

All rights reserved.

No part of this book may be reproduced in any form or by any electronic or mechanical means, including information storage and retrieval systems, without written permission from the author, except for the use of brief quotations in a book review.

A MOUNTAIN
MERMAN
ROMANCE

THE MOUNTAIN MERMAN'S
Curvy Bride

KAT VROMAN

1
Lachlan

I WAKE to my phone ringing by the side of my head.

Oof, I fell asleep reading on the couch again. Merman-strength or not, I was getting too old for anything but a high-quality mattress.

"Hey, what's up?"

"Did I seriously wake you? Aren't you up with the cows, typically?"

"I don't have any cows," I grumble, rubbing my eyes. "Are you calling for a reason?"

"Yeah, I am coming by later today, with someone. It's important you be there so we can talk."

I mumble an OK and hang up. I prefer my days people-free for the most part, but it's been a while since I've seen my brother Murphy. I wonder who he is bringing.

My cabin on Lake Nereid doesn't have cows, but I do have to get up and feed the chickens.

The crisp morning air greets me in the backyard. I longingly look out at the water as my chickens peck at my feet.

I feel an urge to take a quick swim, so I walk down to the bank, slip out of my sweats, and dive right in. The cold water invigorates my foggy mind as my legs and feet shift into a long, strong, purple fishtail. I race the length of the lake several times before getting out to eat breakfast.

A six egg omelet later, I dress and head out to my wood shack to split some logs. The Spring day warms the air as my woodpile increases and I strip off my flannel. As I work up a good sweat, a voice behind me breaks my focus.

"As you can see, Madame Liora, my brother is a beast of a man. I can imagine many women would sleep peacefully next to so much muscle."

"Ah, brother. I expected you later."

I toss down the ax, grab my flannel, and wipe my face down.

"Lachlan, I would like you to meet Madame Liora. She is a matchmaker that I have hired."

As I walk over to shake the strange woman's hand, I size her up. This is a quick feat as she barely stands a full five feet. She stares at me with vibrant violet blue eyes and her hair is long and silver in color.

"It is nice to meet you," Liora says as she shakes my hand.

She then closes her eyes for a long moment, without letting go. I look at Murphy in confusion but he nods at me, indicating I should go with it.

Once she lets go, I invite them in for a drink. We settle on my back patio, watching the chickens do their thing with the lake sparkling in the background. I clear my throat.

"OK, Murphy, spill it. What is a matchmaker?"

"Ah, yes. Well, as you know, when I married Mair I became prince of the merpeople. I am expected to take over for the King once he gives his OK."

I nod. Murphy grew up on Ravenhart Mountain with me and our brothers, Carlow and Beck. But, once he fell for Princess Mair, he left the mountain to live with his bride and her family in the merpeople capitol in the Pacific. He is being groomed to become the future king.

"Well, my father-in-law has informed me that he won't deem me ready for the crown until my side of the family is more robust.

Our parents are gone. I am the only one married. Mair and I have the twins but the King would like to see my brothers married, with children, before giving his blessing on the transfer of power."

I stare at my brother. Is he about to ask me to get married and produce a litter of merspawn?

"So, brother, I have hired Madame Liora here to help with this large endeavor."

Liora smiles up at me. Her eyes are not only beautiful but promise a kindness I am not used to. She begins to speak to me.

"Lachlan, I live at the foot of this mountain in Branwen Beach. I come from a family of witches and I personally practice tactile magic."

I look at my brother, who is smiling at me in a way I think he believes is encouraging. Liora continues.

"What I can do is read people when I touch their hands with mine. Along with guiding spells, I am able to locate this person's true love mate. This process has a mind of its own so I cannot predict how long it will take. I've found mates within an hour before and a couple of times it took me years."

"Years?" Murphy blanches.

"I did warn you, prince, that a true love's match could take time."

"Yes, madame, you did. Sorry to interrupt."

"Lachlan, I pride myself in making matches that are purely a combination of true love and best fit. Even if the two people are very different in multiple ways, I am able to determine that they are meant to be together. If you can place your trust in me like your brother here, I would be happy to help you find your partner in life."

Madame Liora looks at me over her steaming cup of tea, apparently waiting for me to say something.

I have to admit to myself, I was not against falling in love. I just never met anyone I found interesting for more than a couple of weeks and I'm pretty sure those women could have said the same about me. I like living on my own up here on the mountain.

I am happy. But I could also be happy sharing this life with the right woman. I clear my throat.

"I don't see the harm in you trying. And I'll always be there for my brothers. Madame Liora, let's do this."

I reach my hands toward her and she grasps them across the table. She closes her eyes and smiles slightly. After a couple of minutes, she stands up.

"Perfect, I got what I needed," Liora turns to Murphy, "we can go visit your brother Beck now."

Murphy is brimming with excitement and slaps my back.

"Thank you, brother, you've always been good to me."

After they leave, I walk out to the lake and take a long swim. I have to admit to myself, I am a little excited at the prospect of falling hard for someone.

It'll be a first.

2

Paige

THE SHOP DOOR bell rings and I look up to see a purple-haired young woman walk in. I welcome her, point out the sales shelf, and leave her to browse.

My first month as a new business owner is coming to a close and my bookshop has been blessed with an uptick of customers day after day. The month had been successful enough that I was able to hire an employee who is starting tomorrow.

I look over to the framed photo of my grandmother, a tough but loving woman who raised me since birth, and place my hand on the bottom of the frame. I close my eyes and take a couple of deep breaths in, counting the many ways I am grateful for where my life is now.

A year ago I was in a toxic relationship with a man who berated me and laughed at my dreams. We had gotten together a couple of years prior, right when my grandmother passed away. I was swept away by Gary while wallowing in my grief. He love-bombed me with gifts, fancy dinners, and weekends away. We eventually moved in together and that's when he began depriving me of support and love. He was an expert gaslighter and it took me until three months ago to finally walk out on him.

And, boy, did I. I not only walked out on him but I moved

hundreds of miles away to this whimsical beach town at the foot of Ravenhart Mountain.

Branwen Beach was small but bustling due to the regular beautiful weather. Often a stop on travelers' journeys up and down the coast of California, it seemed like a good place for me to start a new life. Ocean breezes, a close-knit community that welcomes outsiders, and in need of a bookshop.

I open my eyes and smile at my grandmother's photo. I know she would be proud of me here.

The bell jingles again and I greet a tiny, elderly woman with long, silver hair. She walks up to the counter and I am taken aback by the color of her eyes. A violet blue that fills me with warmness immediately.

"Welcome to Turn the Paige. How may I help you?"

"I keep meaning to pop in and am finally making the time. What an adorable bookstore you have here. I was wondering what books you have on bread making?"

I show her the cookbook section and point out a couple of good books for new bakers. I leave her to peruse and when she returns to the counter she has an armful of books.

"Wow! You mean business!"

"I couldn't choose. But that's OK, I am very happy to support a locally woman-owned business. My name is Liora, welcome to Branwen Beach."

I ring her up as she tells me about how much she has loved living here the last couple of decades. Liora looks to be in her 70s but she has a youthful energy about her. Once I bag up her books, she thanks me, and heads to the front door but then turns back.

"Oh! I just had a splendid idea. I am hosting the next women's book club at my home on Sunday. I would love for you to join us and meet the other ladies. All ferocious readers. I think they would adore you."

I immediately agree. I have not had a chance to be very social so far, with starting up the business and getting unpacked. Plus this seems like a good idea for the shop. We exchange information and she waves as she heads out the door.

On Sunday afternoon, I knock on Liora's cottage door. Laughter and voices are coming from the back of the house. A woman around my age answers.

"Oh, you must be Paige. Liora said you were joining us. Please come in. I am Fernanda."

Fernanda leads me to the backyard garden, which is set up for tea. She announces my arrival and the women warmly greet me. Liora bounces up to me, clasps my hands, and exclaims how happy she is that I have joined them.

But as soon as the words leave her mouth, her eyes go wide, and she looks deep into my own.

"Are you OK, Liora?" I ask, not sure what her reaction means.

"One moment, please," she replies, closing her eyes and taking a few deep breaths. She reopens them and says, "Sorry, I just had a beautiful moment right then with you. I am very happy you are here and I hope you can linger a bit afterwards so we can chat a bit."

I nod, a little confused by what just happened. But Liora's eyes continue to be filled with warmth and safety, so my confusion turns to curiosity and I take a seat.

After the book club ends, I offer to help clean up. Liora shoos everyone else home, telling them we have it covered.

In her sunshine yellow kitchen, I wash the dishes while she dries and puts them away. We work in silence for a while until she interrupts the quiet.

"Paige, how much do you know about Branwen Beach?"

"Well, I did research before I moved here. I know it's a close-knit community, but still very welcoming of outsiders. And I know many folks with supernatural abilities settle down here because of the accepting culture."

I have a feeling that's what her question was getting at - whether or not I understood that Branwen Beach was a paranormal safe haven.

Liora smiles and says, "Wonderful, I had a feeling you weren't oblivious. I ask because I wanted to share that I am one of those supernatural folks."

Liora pauses, studying me, then continues.

"I have the ability to read people by touching their hands with mine. Typically, it's just getting a feel for their personality. But I am also a matchmaker. People seek me to find their one true love. Their true partner for this life."

I take a sharp breath in. Her reaction when she grasped my hands now made more sense.

"Did you sense something with me, Liora?"

"Yes, yes I did. I guess I wasn't very shy about it," she laughs then continues, "if you allow me to share my knowledge with you, I know who your one true love is. Your perfect mate."

I stand there, holding a soapy plate, staring down at this tiny woman with violet blue eyes. She looks at me in earnest. I realize that I instinctively trust her. I can't explain it with words but I do trust her.

"Do tell."

3

Lachlan

I stand at my front window, looking to see if anyone was coming up my drive yet. Madame Liora called me yesterday, excited that she found my match. I have to admit, I expected this to take longer. I pride myself in my ability to keep my head on my shoulders but right now my stomach feels like butterflies were playing Twister in there.

Madame Liora informed me she would bring what we would need to have a nice first date since we are meeting at my cabin. I am not sure why she suggested the date occur here but I'm happy to not have to drive into town. As for my match, I was told her name and that she owned a bookshop. That is it.

Two cars come rambling up my drive, Liora leading the way. I open the door and watch the two women walk up my front path. A tiny but friendly old woman and the most stunning woman I have ever set eyes upon.

As Paige walks toward me, I attempt to not gawk at her beauty and gorgeous figure. Her wavy, shoulder length hair is the color of cinnamon. She appears to be close to 6 feet in height, with long, shapely legs. Her large breasts are hugged tightly by the t-shirt she is wearing. Her hips as well, underneath a snug, long skirt. Our eyes meet and neither of us appear to be able to look away.

At the doorway, Liora looks between the two of us and gives a small giggle.

"OK, I think you two know who each of you are. Here's a picnic basket filled with goodies and a picnic blanket. I threw in a loaf of bread. I hope it came out OK!"

I think I respond with a thank you but I'm not entirely sure.

"Please come in."

Paige walks across my entrance way, smiling at me. Liora places the basket and blanket inside the doorway, waves, and closes the door behind her. Her car starts up immediately and I hear her drive off my property. I turn to Paige, who is looking around my living room.

"Your home is gorgeous. I love the wood."

"Thank you."

We stare at each other awkwardly. There's an electricity between us. I fight the urge to kiss her right here and now. I clear my throat.

"Well, it's beautiful outside. The lake is behind the house. We could picnic on the shore."

"I would love that."

Liora not only can read people, she also knows how to pack a picnic basket. Wine, cheeses, bread, fruit, and various meats. Paige and I tuck into the lunch, taking turns asking each other questions.

"That's a boring answer. I'm an accountant."

Paige chokes and once she recovers, she replies, "Seriously? I totally thought it would have been something physical. You're so, um, strong looking."

Her cheeks turn pink and she looks down at her plate. I reach out to her arm and give it a squeeze. Paige looks up at me with surprise, breathing in sharply.

"Did you feel that?" she asks.

I had. When I touched her skin it was as if a sparkler went off in between us. The feeling didn't hurt but it did burn. Hot sparks shot through my body.

I close the gap in between us and look down into her dark, brown eyes. I want to kiss her. My body insists upon kissing her.

"Lachlan," she breathes out, looking at me intensely.

I start to lean in, breathing in her scent, letting it consume me. She smells like honey, fresh pages of a book, and chamomile. And human.

I sit up.

"Paige? You're a human?"

Paige looks at me, clearly disappointed that I did not kiss her.

"Yes, I am. Liora told me you are not but she did not elaborate. She thought you should be the one to explain to me."

Paige sits up straighter, her eyes imploring me to share.

I had not even thought that my match would be a human. I was so enthralled with her when she came to my door that my usual instincts were too clouded by my intense desire. Fear grips me. This woman, who I know I am meant to be with, may reject me now. I stand up.

"Lachlan? Are you leaving? Please don't go. I want to know you, the real you."

Paige stands up directly in front of me and places her hand on my chest.

"I realize this may not be what you signed up for," I state, as I start unbuttoning my shirt.

Paige swallows hard as I let the shirt drop to the ground.

"I will show you what I am but you may want to look away. I have to take off my pants as well."

Paige stares at me intensely, her cheeks flushed, and whispers, "I don't want to look away."

Our eyes don't leave each other as I undo my jeans and let them fall to the ground. Next goes my boxers. Paige's breath catches as she allows her eyes to wander down to my hard cock. I can't help it. That electrical touch woke up every inch of my body. She looks back up at me and a hoarse whisper comes out of her soft, full lips.

"Show me who you are."

I walk to the edge of the lake and rush in. The water chills my body for a moment but as soon as I shift into merman form I feel at home. Paige runs to the edge of the lake and waves at me, a huge grin across her face. No one has ever looked at me like this before. I swim around for her, plunge deep, and then breach into the air. I hear laughter and Paige shouting.

"Holy shit!"

I shift back into human form and slowly walk back to her on the land. Paige runs up to me and grabs the sides of my face.

"I have never seen anything so beautiful."

"Are you sure?"

I sound gruff, I realize. I am so out of my element with this woman.

"Damn right I'm sure."

Paige stands before me and lightly touches my dripping wet chest. She looks up at me and says, "I want to kiss you. May I kiss you?"

I think I answer but the next thing I know our lips are pressing together, hungry and frantic. She opens her mouth for me and I slide my tongue in, tasting strawberries and wine. Her large breasts are pressed up against me, with her shirt wet from my body. I explore her chin, neck, and clavicle with my mouth and tongue as she moans softly in my ear. I am aware of nothing but her body. I slide my hand over her covered nipple, feeling it harden with my touch. Paige's moans become stronger but are suddenly interrupted with a loud thunderclap.

We both look up, surprised. Dark clouds have taken the sunny day away and fat drops of rain start to pelt us. Paige shrieks as the rain starts coming down in buckets. I grab her hand and we race back up to the cabin.

4

Paige

I HAVE NEVER BEEN SO TURNED on by a man as I am with Lachlan Atwater.

I would have expected his transformation into a merman before my eyes to amaze me but I did not expect my panties to become wet. As he walked back to me on the shore, my pussy started throbbing. Lachlan stood before me, naked, dripping wet, and chiseled. His cock was just as hard as it was before he jumped into the water. I wanted to swirl my tongue around it and make him groan.

I've never made the first move with a guy before but I knew this man belonged to me. I must have him. Taste him.

And taste him I did. Lachlan's lips were flavored like red wine and salt from the cheese. I pressed into him, enjoying his mouth explore my neck while his hands woke up my nipples. Then the sky opened up and fell on our heads.

In the living room, we watch the rain come down in sheets. Lachlan mutters about how the storm was supposed to miss us and go North but apparently the meteorologists got this one wrong. He covers up his firm ass and thick length with a throw blanket from the couch then starts a fire.

"You're shivering. I am going to draw you a bath."

"Th-th-thank you," I say, through chattering teeth.

The soak warms me to my bones. I dry off and throw on the flannel shirt he left me. It wears like a short dress. He also left me warm wool socks. This guy has a gruff exterior but he sure knows how to take care of me.

I return to the living room to find him dressed and listening to the radio.

"The road you take off the mountain is washed out. It's not safe for you to go home today."

"Oh."

I feel a bit awkward. I have no idea if Lachlan is OK with me staying over when we literally just met.

"You'll take my bed and I'll take the couch."

I can't help but laugh. There's no way this 6' 5" man can comfortably sleep on this couch.

"I'll take the couch. I am not kicking you out of your own bed."

Lachlan opens his mouth to respond when the lights go out. The storm continues to rage outside, providing little light. He shuffles in a drawer and sets up some candles.

"OK, well, I am not having a lady sleep on my couch. Although, now that the electricity is out it may also get cold in here. This fireplace only provides so much heat."

I can't believe I am about to offer this, since we just met, but I suggest, "Why don't we both sleep in the bed. We can have our own blankets but our body heat should also help keep us warm?"

Lachlan looks at me, a brief moment of hunger flashes in his eyes.

"I will be a gentleman, of course. I think that's probably the best idea. Let me find some extra blankets before it gets even darker."

The lights do not come back on so we head to bed early. My entire body feels alive knowing he's within touching distance but I tell myself that even though we have been matched we shouldn't throw caution to the wind. The rain continues to come down hard outside.

"I love the sound of rain," I admit, quietly, into the dark.

"Me too."

I feel him shift so that he seems to be facing me.

"Do you come down the mountain a lot?"

"Only when I have to. My brother Murphy lives in the water near your town but my other two brothers live up here."

We talk into the night. Lachlan has a dry sense of humor that cracks me up. At one point, mid-laugh, I feel his hand reach out to me. I take it and we lie on the bed in silence. The rain is slowing down outside, dancing on the window. My eyes grow heavy.

I wake to a weak light coming in through the window. We are no longer holding hands. Both of us shifted during the night. I get up and tiptoe to the bathroom.

When I come out, Lachlan is sitting up in bed. The morning light illuminates the muscles on his bare chest and I catch my breath.

"I don't understand how Liora knew I'd fall for you," I blurt out.

"You've fallen for me?"

Lachlan smiles at me and gets out of bed. He walks to where I stand and pulls my hips toward him.

"Yes. I don't know how she knew but you're the man for me, Lachlan Atwater."

He tilts my chin up and brushes his lips across mine.

We kiss each other hungrily as he fumbles with the buttons of my flannel. My shirt falls to the floor and Lachlan takes in my naked body with the eyes of a famished wolf.

"Damn, you're breathtaking," he whispers as he takes my nipple into his mouth.

I moan loudly as he sucks and licks my nipple while lightly pinching the other one. I slowly sit on the bed and guide him onto me. He squeezes my tits together, licking back and forth between each nipple while grinding his rock hard bulge in between my thighs. I try to shimmy his gray sweatpants off but he holds up a finger.

"Hold on, boo, I need to explore some more first."

Lachlan slowly kisses down my round stomach, mumbling about how soft my skin is. He kisses the insides of my thighs and lightly bites them with his lips. He takes his big, strong hands and pushes my knees open while dropping his open mouth onto my pussy.

"Holy," I moan out when he starts to twirl his tongue around my clit. He sucks on it, flicking it with his rhythmic tongue. He is reading my body's reactions. I am loudly praising a god I don't believe in when my orgasm comes crashing down all over me. My knees clamp shut and he pries his head free, laughing.

"Oh no, I'm sorry," I giggle into his shoulder when he scooches up to me on the bed.

"Are you kidding? Nearly getting my head popped off is quite the compliment," Lachlan's hazel eyes crinkled as he grins at me.

I start kissing him, getting up on my knees.

"OK, sir, time to retire the sweatpants."

After I pull off his pants, I climbed on top of him, sliding my wet pussy along his hard shaft. Back and forth, getting a little closer to his head entering into me each time.

"You tease," he says in a husky voice, slapping my round ass.

"I do," I respond as I slide his cock into me. Lachlan lets out a long groan.

As I ride him, my heavy breasts bounce while he hungrily watches them. I lean forward and he takes one in his mouth, sucking my nipple in deep. I grind his length deeper into me, feeling another orgasm build. Lachlan grabs my hips and starts pounding me down onto him. He takes one hand to turn my face to him, we meet eyes, and we come together while yelling out.

Untangling our bodies, breathing heavy, we softly giggle and snuggle into each other. I know I need to get back down the mountain today once the road is cleared but I'm not in a rush.

5
Lachlan

Both Paige and I had work responsibilities the next few days. I keep myself busy with my clients' work but the days drag by until our evening phone calls. Each night I start a fire, pour myself an Irish whiskey, and settle down to chat with her about anything and nothing. We once even stream a show together and call it a date.

I don't quite understand how someone so full of light is into me. Paige definitely brings out a softer, sunnier version of myself but I am still me. And it is me who she apparently has fallen hard for. A month ago I didn't even think about dating and now here I am, absolutely smitten.

Thursday evening we make plans for Saturday. I offer to come down to her but Paige says she is fine coming here. When we hang up I see that my Friday client emailed to cancel our meetings for the day due to a family emergency. Perfect, I think. I can surprise Paige at her shop.

In the morning I head down the mountain and stop at Poppy's flower shop.

"Well color me shocked, an Atwater brother down the mountain!" Poppy exclaims as she comes out from the back of the shop.

"Hey, Poppy, long time no see."

"No kidding. How's my former classmate doing? Still being a nerd with numbers?"

"It pays the bills. Hey, Poppy, what type of flowers do you recommend for surprising my girlfriend? It's a new relationship but intense."

Poppy's mouth drops open as she looks me up and down.

"Down the mountain and has a girlfriend? Did I wake up in the UpsideDown this morning?"

I give her a look and she gets busy behind the flower case.

"OK, fine Lachlan. Well, since it's all new may I suggest tulips? Perfect for Spring and very romantic for a budding relationship."

"Deal, let's do it."

I park on Main Street and head to the corner I know her bookstore is on. The attached cafe is still empty but the market across the street seems to be getting good business.

Turn the Paige stands before me. It has the look of a whimsical cottage on the outside, with vines, flowers, and gnome figurines. I smile to myself. This place screams Paige to me. I love it.

I walk into the shop and a little bell jingles above my head. Paige is standing with her back to me. She is talking closely to a man in front of her who is smiling at her and touching her arm. He catches my eye.

"Can we help you?"

Paige turns, seeing me, and her mouth drops slightly open.

"I'm here to see Paige. I can wait until she's done."

"And who might you be?" the man gives an air of protectiveness and ownership.

Who is this guy?

"I doubt that's your concern. You can finish your business."

"Gary," Paige says in a tired voice but the man ignores her and stomps up closer to me.

"It is my god damn concern, buddy. That's my girlfriend. Who the fuck are you?!"

I look from this Gary asshole to Paige. Her eyes are huge and tears are welling up in them. Gary stands in front of me with his arms crossed. My temper flares.

"A fricken boyfriend? What is this shit?" I demand, throwing the flowers on the floor and storming out the door.

In the sunshine, I don't know what to do with myself. I am too angry to drive so I heft it to the beach, cursing every little thing.

What a sucker I was. I can't believe I fell for this matchmaking bullshit. Of course there wasn't an incredible, sexy, curvy woman out there who is perfect for me. What a fool I am. Paige was just playing a game with me.

Once I reach the ocean I pick up rocks from the sand and pelt them into the waves. I shout some selected curse words into the salty wind.

"Dude, are you having an actual mantrum?" a voice yells out to me.

Murphy is sitting on a jetty in his merman form, watching me with bemusement. He swims over, walks out of the water butt naked, and throws on a robe that was laying on the beach.

"Paige has a fucking boyfriend."

"What? No she doesn't. Well, I mean, minus you."

"I literally just met him, Murph. He's a prick. I was an idiot to believe in this magical matchmaking Liora crap."

"Listen, dude, she does not have a boyfriend. Liora and I have been in contact this whole time. Paige literally moved here to start a new life to get away from a toxic ex. Larry, Jerry, I don't know."

"Gary?"

"Maybe?"

Fuck. I am an idiot but not for the reason I thought.

"I got to go."

I run off from Murphy who laughs while yelling good luck to me.

When I reach the bookstore's door I find it locked even though the sign says Open. I bang on the door. No response but I can hear a muffled argument. I bang again and wait. Something is wrong. I can feel it in my core. I begin kicking at the door. The third kick cracks it off the hinges.

"Paige?" I shout, throwing the door to the side.

Voices are coming from the room behind the register.

I rush to the back and find Gary pressed up against Paige. I step forward to grab him when she manages to free her hands and pushes him hard toward me. Gary falls against my chest. I grab his neck and slam him to the wall.

"Lachlan!"

"Paige, is this guy bothering you?"

"Yes! He's not my boyfriend. He's my piece of shit ex."

Gary tries to squirm away from my grip but I have several inches and several pounds of muscle on him. I grip his collar and drag him to the front of the shop.

"I better not fucking see you around these parts ever again, dick."

I toss him down the front steps and he lays splayed out on the sidewalk.

"Get lost!"

Gary jumps up, runs to a beat up Chrysler, hops in, and peels out.

I turn to see Paige standing behind me with her arms crossed, looking at her broken door with tears in her eyes.

"You can leave, too, Lachlan. I don't know why the hell you don't trust me after the connection we've experienced but you need to get the hell out of my store."

I open my mouth to protest but her face fills with hurt fury and she points to the door.

"Out! I want to be alone."

6
Paige

My new employee, Rex, offers to spend the night in the shop to keep out any stragglers.

"Are you sure? I can camp out here."

"No, ma'am. Boy, my ma would be angry if I let a woman spend the night in a shop without a door."

I smile. This day has been pure shit but Rex has been a gem.

"OK, but please call me if anything happens or you need me to take over."

At home, I take a long, hot shower. Gary showing up at my work scared me. Lachlan assuming the worst of me scared me as well. I was mad at him for believing Gary's bullshit so quickly. I realize we had not discussed my ex yet but I refused to be OK with his angry reaction.

I dry off and get into my pajamas. Normally this was the time Lachlan and I would chat on the phone but I decide to watch a Dateline instead.

Dateline probably wasn't the best choice but it did make me think. Gary had busted in demanding I come back to him. He had lost his job and apparently realized I was good to keep around to pay the bills. I don't know how far he would have taken his attack on me but I am grateful that Lachlan returned when he did.

After the episode, I step out onto my patio and take a few long drags off my vape. I need to end this day and get some good sleep.

I stop at the donut shop near my place and grab coffee and donuts to share with Rex. It's a perfect Spring day and I feel my mood lifting as I walk down Main Street. I see Donna sweeping the steps outside her market and stop to chat.

"Nice new door you got there," she says cheerfully to me.

"New door?"

I look across the street at my store and see a brand new door has been installed.

Donna laughs.

"Did you forget? Looks like it's quite intricate! I'll stop by later to admire it closer."

I check both ways and run across the street. The door looks to be oak, with mythological creatures carved into it. It's absolutely gorgeous.

"Uh, Rex?" I call out, hands too full to knock.

"Ma'am!" Rex opens the door, "Look at what Mr. Atwater installed. Isn't it a beaut?"

"Mr. Atwater?"

"Hey," Lachlan comes out from behind the book stacks.

"Rex, here, go enjoy these donuts at home. Thank you so much for keeping an eye on the place last night."

Rex pops a donut between his teeth and mumbles "no problem" as he leaves.

"I brought you these as well."

Lachlan hands me a bouquet of tulips, similar to what I saw him throw on the ground yesterday, but even bigger.

"Lachlan..."

"I know it doesn't make up for my behavior but you deserve beautiful flowers. Hell, you deserve everything. I behaved like a stupid ass and I'm sorry. I am so used to being on my own and I let my temper take control. Which is absolutely no excuse. I should have known to trust the woman I'm in love with and I am really sorry I did not."

Lachlan heads to the door to leave.

"Wait."

He turns and looks at me with eyes full of regret.

"What you did was not OK. That's not something I will ever tolerate. Gary is the last toxic man I will ever share a life with, OK?"

"OK, yes, definitely. I am better than the man I was yesterday. And you sure as hell deserve the best I can offer."

"What is that exactly? The best you can offer?"

Lachlan walks over to me and brushes a stray strand of hair behind my ear.

"First of all, I will trust you and always assume best intentions. I will love and support you. Hell, I would even move off the mountain if it meant being with you."

A small gasp leaves my lips and I shake my head.

"I would never in a million years ask you to do such a thing. It's only a half hour to my shop."

Lachlan smiles at me.

"I don't think I could love you more but I also know I will love you more each and every day. Paige, you're the one for me. Even if you reject my love, I will never get over it."

I wrap my arms around his middle and pull him closer.

"You keep mentioning this love word."

"I love you, Paige Solberg. Now and forever."

I go up on my tiptoes, our noses almost touching.

"I love you too, Lachlan Atwater. Now and forever."

His hand reaches behind my head and our mouths meet. The kiss is long and deep and his hand fists the back of my hair. I press my body against him and feel his arousal.

"What time do you open?"

"Not for another half hour, lock the door," I purr as I let my panties fall to the floor.

When he walks back to me I unzip him, yank his jeans down, while leading him to a chair against the wall. I hike my skirt up and straddle him on the chair. This time I do not tease. I slide him right in. I ride his cock hard as he throws off my t-shirt. He pinches my nipples hard through the lace of my bra and buries his face into my cleavage. We come undone together in a sweaty, happy mess.

Chapter 7
Lachlan

"I have no idea what I should wear."

Paige stands in front of her closet, wearing just a silk slip, frantically looking through her dresses. I watch her, amused, sitting on the edge of her bed.

"Boo, it truly doesn't matter. Murphy and Mair are just excited to meet you."

"Prince Murphy. Princess Mair. How soon you forget."

I laugh and pull her onto my lap.

"My beautiful Paige, they're just people. Well, merpeople, whatever. And I think they're more concerned about impressing my human girlfriend than anything else."

Paige rolls her eyes and laughs.

"OK, fine, but I still need a dress that will go with the air mask I have to wear. I guess I should go the classic route. Little black dress it is."

"Good choice. That will look good on the floor later tonight."

My brother lives in the underwater capitol with his wife, twins, and her royal family. Our dinner is being held in an underwater cave where they can adjust the temperature to make it more comfortable for Paige. And Liora, who is invited as well as a thank you for her work.

Murphy and Mair greet us with love and warmth. Murphy relays that his father-in-law is pleased with the match and looks forward to Beck and Carlow finding mates as well.

We feast on lobster, clams, seaweed salad, and scallops. Seawater wine is aplenty and Paige is amazed at the unique flavor.

"Unfortunately, you cannot enjoy this on land. It spoils once it hits the air," Mair shares as she pours us new glasses.

Liora takes her glass and stands up.

"I would like to toast the new couple. To true love, true partnership, and true connection!"

We clink glasses while laughing and continue to enjoy the evening.

Paige and I stand on the beach after dinner, looking out at the dark waves. The night has been perfect and the two of us have an air of satisfaction surrounding us. I had been waiting for the perfect moment and, here I was, suddenly standing in it.

I drop to one knee and take a box out of my jacket pocket.

"Lachlan!"

Paige's hand flies to her mouth.

"Paige, I have never met a woman like you. You are absolute sunshine in human form. You have enriched my life in a way I could not have imagined a year ago. I am madly, passionately, desperately in love with you and I want to spend the rest of my days with you. Will you marry me?"

Tears fall down her cheeks and Paige exclaims, "Yes! Yes!"

I stand up and lift her into my arms. As I lower her, we kiss deeply.

"Before I put this ring on your finger, there is one more thing we need to do."

"What's that?"

"Well, I'm a merman. You're a human. We will often find ourselves underwater. Since you are my true love, I can offer you my merman's kiss. The kiss will protect you from drowning for the rest of your life."

"Well then, come here, big fella."

I place my hands on the sides of Paige's face and draw her close to me. This kiss is like no other we have experienced so far or will ever experience again. I feel her skin's temperature heat up in my hands and she feels like she is about to float into the air. When I break the seal, she stares up at me and mouths the word, "Wow."

Epilogue
Paige

I CRANK up the shop's air conditioning.

"I am officially over Summer," I announce to Lachlan and Rex.

Lachlan reaches around my waist and pulls me to him.

"Now now, fiancee, don't shoo the Summer away just yet. I have a bride to marry in this Summer heat."

"Oh really? Well, I suppose I can be a little more patient."

Rex laughs at us and looks out the window.

"Oh wow, someone is finally moving into the cafe next door."

Lachlan and I peer out the window with him and see a short, thin woman carrying boxes into the cafe.

"Rex, will you mind the store? Lachlan, let's go help her."

Outside, the Summer heat is oppressive unless an ocean breeze blows by. The woman is standing by her truck, chugging water.

"Hi there, welcome. I'm the owner next door," I walk up to the woman, giving a friendly wave.

"Oh hi. Sorry, I'm a sweaty mess. Nice to meet you. I'm Dulce,"

Dulce shakes my hand.

"I'm Paige and this is my almost husband, Lachlan."

"Why hello there, Almost Husband."

"Howdy. I'm going to send my Almost Wife back into her air conditioned store but I would be happy to help you bring in some boxes. What are you going to do with the place?"

"It will be a bakery. I've worked in bakeries all my life but this will be the first one to call my own."

I open my mouth to say something but hear a familiar voice calling from across the street.

"Look who it is, the happy bride and groom!"

Liora calls out from in front of the market and walks over to our side.

"Liora! This is my new neighbor. She's opening a bakery next door. Dulce, please meet Liora, a budding bread maker."

"Oh cool, I love baking bread."

Dulce reaches out her hand to Liora. When Liora grasps it in return, her eyes go wide. She looks sharply at me.

"Paige, you have room for one more at your wedding on Saturday, correct?"

I look back at her, a little startled that she would invite a stranger to my wedding. But Liora's eyes say it all.

"Of course! What a fantastic idea. Please, Dulce, join us on Saturday. It will be a great party and you can meet many folks from town."

"Oh my goodness, that's so friendly. Sure, that sounds like a lot of fun to be honest."

Lachlan clears his throat.

"OK, Almost Wife, get back into the A/C. You know this heat wears you down."

"Fine, Almost Husband, but as soon as you're done helping Dulce then it's time for you to finish writing your vows."

"Gladly, I have a lot to say," Lachlan kisses me and sends me back into the shop.

Kat Vroman

A MOUNTAIN
MERMAN
ROMANCE

THE
MOUNTAIN
MERMAN'S
Love Connection

KAT VROMAN

1

Dulce

I am falling asleep on my feet.

I stare around at my new bakery. The glass cases arrived today, although now they were difficult to see in the swarm of stacked boxes. The adorable bistro table sets I ordered will arrive tomorrow and, before I go home, I need to make some space. An afternoon wedding invitation limits my morning time.

I barely stepped foot into Branwen Beach when I met my insanely tall but friendly neighbors. Well, my business neighbors. Paige owns the adorable bookshop next to me. Tomorrow she is marrying Lachlan, a beast of a mountain man - lordy. They invited me to the wedding after this wisp of a woman with long, silver hair essentially forced their hand. I was about to be horrified and decline, but Paige genuinely appeared excited to include me.

I'm never one to say no to an adventure.

I make quick work of creating space for the table sets and lock up. I rented an apartment down the street. It is a simple studio above a pizza parlor, but it is perfect for right now. I ran over to turn on the air conditioning a couple of hours ago and it will be a perfect icebox. This California heat wave is no joke.

Moxie, my American shorthair, greets me at the door. By

greets I mean yells at me to feed her. I comply since she's the boss of the house.

After stumbling over some moving boxes, I make it into the shower to wash the grime and sweat off me. I had planned to search my boxes for a dress for tomorrow, but I can no longer keep my eyes open. I don't even bother opening up my futon. As soon as I lie down, Moxie claims her spot on my hip, and I fall into a deep sleep.

In the morning, I drink my caramel coffee and destroy the boxes packed with my wardrobe. My X-Men skill today is apparently finding every piece of clothing I own, minus anything suitable for a wedding. I swear I owned dresses that were not just for renaissance fairs, but I am apparently wrong.

After I hang up my ren fair beauties, I hop onto my laptop to see what clothing stores are nearby. I admittedly did not research Branwen Beach before moving here, minus knowing they had space for a new bakery.

Well, and that they would accept me here. I would be safe.

I find a store down the street that has potential. I give Moxie an ear scratch goodbye, throw a baseball cap on to hide my bird's nest, and walk to the shop.

Rainbow's Eclectics is exactly that. The store is full of eclectic pieces of clothing, with no theme, rhyme, or reason. Flashes of color pop out amongst blacks, grays, and browns. A bell tinkles as I enter and a woman with short, blue hair greets me.

"Welcome! How can I help you?"

"I am looking for a dress that's appropriate for a wedding I am going to tonight."

"Oh, you wouldn't happen to be going to Lachlan's wedding by any chance?"

"Yes. I don't know the couple well, I just bought the bakery next to his fiancee's bookshop, and they were kind enough to invite me."

"Lachlan and his family have always been good people. I grew up with them. I'll be there tonight, too. I'm Rain. Let me show you some of our dresses that I think would look amazing on that petite figure of yours."

An hour later, I leave the shop with the most darling dress. Rain understood my fashion sense after a brief conversation. I chose a sleeveless, a-line sheer dress with a plunging neckline. It is stunning, if I do say so myself. The aquamarine color brings out the green in my hazel eyes, and my white sandals will work well for the beach wedding.

I drop off my new threads and head over to the bakery to wait for the bistro table set delivery. Turns out my shop is the delivery truck's first stop, so I have plenty of time to get ready for the late afternoon wedding.

I am surprised I feel a little nervous about tonight. I am always up for a new experience and especially love to travel solo. Tonight has higher stakes for me, I suppose. I will meet people who live in the town I am now calling home. I would like to make a good first impression.

Mid-afternoon, I stand staring at myself in the mirror after putting my hair in a twisted updo. I twirl like a schoolgirl and blow myself a kiss. This will do.

2

Beck

    I step back and look at my model. Mrs. Black is shifted in her cat form, elegantly posing on a seat cushion. I add some color to the eyes to make them glow the way hers do and step back again, clapping my hands together.

    "Ma'am, please take a look. I think you will be pleased."

    Mrs. Black, without warning, shifts before me. I avert my eyes as she places her silk robe over her naked body. Don't get me wrong, she has a great body, but she's my friend's mother.

    She stalks towards me and purrs when she sees the portrait.

    "Beck, my darling, you always have such a keen eye."

    Mrs. Black's fingers play upon my shoulder.

    I step back and thank her.

    "I appreciate the compliment, Mrs. Black. Once it dries, I will wrap it up and drop it off at your husband's office, since that's not too far away from here. I hope that works for you."

    I hear a slow hiss come out of her dark red lips, but she plasters on a smile.

    "That will work. Good day."

    I catch myself holding my breath, which I release out slowly once my studio door closes. If the circumstances had been differ-

The Mountain Merman's Love Connection

ent, I would not mind a romp with a cougar. But I don't betray friends, and I certainly don't interfere with marriages.

I look in the mirror and spot a new gray in my beard. Forty-three is less than a year away so it is what it is. I rub my beard and check over my face. Not too shabby for an old man.

Crap, it's already noon. I need to shower and get my butt to the Branwen Beach Hotel to meet up with the other groomsmen. This best man role is kicking my free-going ass a bit. I'm not sure why Lachlan insisted I be his best man when he knows how artsy fartsy flaky my head can get. But he wouldn't take no for an answer. Love that guy.

In Lachlan's suite, wearing matching beige linen suits, Murphy, Carlow, the bride's brother, Gregory, and I hang around sipping good whiskey while the groom makes some last-minute touches to his getup. I never thought this day would come, that my oldest brother, Mr. Mountain Man Loner, would fall in love and get married.

Of course, he had help. My brother Murphy hired Madame Liora, our local mystical matchmaker, to find true love connections for his siblings. This is a requirement of his father-in-law, the king of the merpeople, before Murphy can succeed him on the throne.

I met Liora in the Spring. She held my hands and read me but I have not heard a peep from her since. I understand it can take years, but the idea of a true love mate excites me. I hope it happens for me like it did for Lachlan. Life on the mountain can be lonely without someone to share it with.

Once Lachlan is ready, we take photos on the beach with the wedding photographer. My brother is beaming. I expected him to have some wedding jitters, but he is the epitome of cool and collected. Paige is his true love mate, and he knows it down to his soul. It is a beautiful sight and part of me wishes I was there as an artist to capture his spirit on canvas.

I stand next to Lachlan up at the altar, the ocean behind us. The sun lowers in the sky as dark yellow rays dance upon the guests sitting in front of us. I spot Liora in the crowd, who is sitting next to a woman I don't recognize. I squint to get a better look, but the processional starts and my attention diverts to the bridesmaids walking down the aisle. Three are relatives on Paige's side and my sister-in-law, Princess Mair, is included as well. Paige has a good eye for colors. The sky blue bridesmaid dresses look amazing with the beach backdrop.

Once the bridesmaids are down the aisle, I peek over at the unfamiliar woman I previously noticed. She is staring at me and quickly looks away when we meet eyes. A spark vibrates through me from head to toe. My breath escapes my lungs and my hand flies up to my chest.

"Dude, you OK?" Lachlan whispers to me.

"Yeah, totally," I lie, right as the guests stand up to watch the bride proceed down the aisle.

3

Dulce

The wedding ceremony makes me cry because, of course, it does. I am such a sucker for romance.

I am also a sucker for good-looking men and, oh my, the groom's brothers offer up some eye candy. From the groom's party of four, it is clear who his brothers are. The three of them tower over 6 feet in height and their suits can not hide the muscle underneath the linen. Not one appears to own a razor, but that just adds to the delicious mountain man look. And when I meet eyes with the best man, my entire body turns to jello.

After the ceremony, I continue to puzzle over my reaction to this brother as the wedding party leads the guests to the water's edge. Music rises around us and a mermaid show amongst the waves begins. I have heard of merpeople but have never met one. Well, until the groom, I suppose.

The show is mesmerizing. Various colors of iridescent scales gleam in the lowering sun rays. The performers put Olympic synchronized swimmers to shame.

Afterwards, the reception takes place at a restaurant on the beach that is a simple walk from the ceremony spot. I am seated at a table with Liora and several women.

"Dulce, I would like you to meet the women from the bride's and my book club. This is Vanessa, Penny, Fernanda, and Rose."

"Nice to meet you all."

"A few other members are here but sitting with their spouses," Liora explains.

My table company is lively. The women actively make me feel welcome by including me in their conversations and asking me questions. Penny gets to the heart of the matter with her first inquiry posed to me.

"So, husband, wife, kids, what's your story?"

I choke on my sip of wine and Liora scolds Penny.

"Leave the poor woman alone, Penny, goodness."

She laughs and shrugs her shoulders at me, but I can tell Liora would also love to know my answer.

"Well, I was married briefly at 18 and we had a baby, my son Sean. His dad and I broke up soon after the birth and his father enlisted in the army. He was good about sending me child support, but I was essentially a single mom until the age of 37. My boy is now an ad exec in New York City. He's doing great. Once he was out of the house, I went to culinary school. After a few years working around the country, I decided to settle down here and run my own bakery."

"Oh, the place next to Paige's shop? That's fantastic. I can't wait until you open!" Vanessa says.

"Me too. It will be nice to not have to climb over moving boxes."

I notice Liora studying my face.

"You look a lot like my older sister Merla did at your age. It's uncanny."

"Oh really? Does she live nearby?" I ask.

"I wish but, no. Neither of my sisters do. Merla lives an adorable beach life with her wife on Cape Cod. I need to visit again soon. Her town is so quaint. My other sister, Sidra, is basically a nomad. She's a gather-no-moss type."

Liora begins to share what her sisters do for work when the cake cutting begins.

After the serving of wedding cake, which is from a famous Los Angeles bakery, Liora offers to walk me around to make introductions. I have a feeling I will be a bit on display, but I knew this was coming. She leads me around the tables and I am already lost in the faces and names. I know I met a couple of schoolteachers. They declared they will be first in line when I open the bakery.

"Now, let me take you up to the wedding party. I know you met the bride and groom, of course, but how about Lachlan's brothers? Have the pleasure yet?"

I nervously clear my throat.

"No, not yet."

Liora starts the introductions as far away from the best man as possible. I am torn between finding it a relief and finding it torture. I meet the prince and his wife, who strike me as average folks who just happen to be royalty. Carlow, the youngest brother, is polite but clearly uncomfortable. I don't think big gatherings are his thing, since he looks like he is itching to bolt out of the restaurant.

Liora tugs on me to follow her to the last brother, the jello maker. As she introduces me to him, he stands up to shake my hand. We stand there, staring at each other, his green eyes practically reading my thoughts. Liora, at least I think it is her, is speaking, but the voice is coming through a muffled haze. I feel someone place my hand into his and the instant spark wakes us both up.

"Whoa, you feel that?" he asks me.

"Yeah, I did. That was some shock."

I look around, and Liora is now on the other side of the dance floor, chatting away.

In fact, the entire wedding party has dissipated. Some making the rounds, a few dancing.

"How long have we been standing here?" I ask the most gorgeous man I have ever laid eyes on.

The brother laughs and looks around.

"Good question, I am not sure. Apparently, we both passed out."

His smile is infectious and causes his laugh lines to become more pronounced. I want to jump him.

Instead, I laugh at his joke. He takes my hand again.

"I think while I was snoozing, I did not catch your name. I'm Beck, Lachlan's younger brother."

"Dulce. I own the bakery next to Paige's shop. I'm new to town. Do you live in Branwen Beach?"

"Nah, I'm a mountain guy. But I'm only 20 minutes up the mountain, so not bad."

I continue to stare at his green eyes like a love-struck fool until he asks me for a dance. We walk to the dance floor and an energy forms between us. I wonder if the other guests can feel it or if it just belongs to us. Every time his hand touches my arms, or my waist, electric currents shoot through my entire body. Beck watches my every move on the dance floor with a look that curls my toes. I don't know what this is, but I want more of it. I want all of it.

During the final slow dance, Beck pulls me close. I can feel that he is as attracted to me as I am to him. I press closer to him and he gently places my head on his chest. We sway there, oblivious to the rest of the dance floor.

Beck whispers in my ear, "Want to take a walk on the beach?"

4

BECK

I hold this petite, vibrant woman in my arms on the dance floor. Dulce stares up at me, her hazel eyes flecked with green. She is beaming at me with her auburn and gray hair framing her delicate features. I want to kiss each freckle on her nose, but I behave myself.

"I would love to go for a walk," Dulce slides her hand into mine.

We head to the coat check. I grab my jacket and ask what she brought.

"Silly me, did not think this far into the night. The day's heat got to me, so I assumed it wouldn't be too chilly now."

We step outside and the ocean breezes prove her wrong. I wrap my linen suit jacket over Dulce's shoulders.

"Thank you, you sure? You're not cold?"

"I don't think I could ever feel cold standing next to you."

Dulce gives a shy giggle and playfully bumps my side with her shoulder. I tower over this woman. She has to be more than a foot shorter than me. But I can tell she's my perfect fit. In my gut, I know this spitfire of a woman is mine.

We hold hands and talk about our lives. I learn about her

adult son in NYC. She learns about my artwork and business on the mountain. I offer to take tomorrow off to help her unpack her bakery.

"Wow, you sure? I don't want to take advantage of your hospitality."

"I'm 100% sure. Hell, I'd be happy watching paint dry with you."

The night is dark, but I can still see Dulce blush and look shyly away.

"Can I ask you a question, Beck?"

"Of course."

"Are you a merman like Lachlan?"

"I sure am."

"Well, then, can I show you something? I have not gotten around to sharing this with anyone here."

I nod, and she steps away from me. Dulce closes her eyes and her dress flutters around her. Sheer cloth twists about her body and forms into gleaming white feathers. In a moment, a regal swan stands in front of me.

"Beautiful!" I can't help but exclaim, "I have never met a swan shifter before."

In my excitement, I unbutton my shirt. I did not realize a swan could appear to hunger for my bare chest, but Dulce's swan sure did.

"I have to take my pants off as well, if you'd like to turn around."

Dulce, however, stays in her spot, so I disrobe in front of her. Her intense stare has made me hard, and I am very aware of how vulnerable I feel in front of her. I give her a small smile and walk into the dark waters, shifting into my merman form once I am deep enough. Dulce's swan swims out to meet me and we play in the waves. She rubs her soft swan's head and neck along my chest. I run my hand down her silky, feathered body.

When we notice the guests leaving the restaurant, we swim to shore. I dress, and she shifts back into her wedding attire. I stand there soaking wet, but she looks the same as before she shifted. She notices me studying her.

"It's part of swan shifter magic. We don't have to get undressed and we don't alter how we look when we shift back."

I take her hand as we walk off the beach.

"Well, I hope you're able to get undressed for other events."

Dulce giggles and gives my hand a squeeze. This woman is divine.

Her apartment is a short walk from the beach. I walk Dulce to her door.

"I am so glad we met tonight. I look forward to seeing you at the bakery tomorrow. What time do you want me?"

"Does 10 work?"

"Perfect, I'll be there." I take her hand, bend down, and kiss it. An electric current spreads across my lips.

"I'll see you tomorrow," she whispers as she goes inside.

Shit. Shit. Shit.

I drive too fast down the mountain road. Holy, I am such an idiot. I woke up with the sunrise and decided to paint until it was time to help Dulce. Stupid, moronic me got swept up in the new art piece and when I looked at the clock, it was past noon.

Shit. Shit. Shit.

I make it to town and force myself to slow down on its streets. Last thing I need is the attention of the sheriff.

Shit. Shit. Shit.

I park on Main Street and hop out of the car. I look down at the mess I am wearing. My shirt and jeans are covered in paint. I am a hot mess.

Shit. Shit. Shit.

I stand in front of her bakery. I am mad at myself for being a fuck up so soon after meeting her. I know she's meant to be mine, and I need to make this right.

When I walk in, Dulce looks up at me from the corner of the shop. She looks tired and sweaty. I can't read her expression, but there's definitely a sprinkling of unimpressed peppered throughout.

"I am so, so sorry."

"What happened?"

She sounds as tired as she looks. I make a mental note not to tell her that.

"I got caught up in an art project I started at 7:00 am. It didn't even occur to me that I would get swept away by it. I should have set an alarm. I'm truly sorry."

Dulce considers me from her corner. She eventually nods.

"Mistakes happen. Thank you for showing up. It's not like you had to."

"I am a man of my word, even if I come late like a fool. Have you eaten?"

Once she tells me no, I hurry off to buy lunch at a sandwich shop. When I return, I insist she take a break and nourish her tired body. Of course, I don't mention the tired part.

I encourage her to rest longer than the time it takes to eat the sandwich and ask her to tell me what needs to be done. Dulce has perked up from the food and we make it into a game - me guessing where things go and her letting me know if I guessed right. The hours to sunset go by fast. We are laughing and easily enjoying ourselves. I'm relieved she forgave my screw up.

"Beck, you're amazing. But I must insist you head home. It's getting dark."

"Yes, ma'am. That's probably a good idea."

We linger by the front door. I lean a shoulder against the frame and cross my arms while looking down into her irresistible face.

"Would you allow me the honor of taking you out for dinner tomorrow night? Do you like sushi?"

"I love sushi," Dulce smiles up at me.

I feel my skin go hot looking down at her petite body.

"Perfect. Is 5:00 too early? Just thinking about the light."

"Works for me. I have a good relationship with my boss."

I give her a big grin before taking my leave. Dulce lightly touches my elbow as a goodbye.

I whistle back to my car. This woman has me bewitched and I would not have it any other way.

I knock on her apartment door and hand her a bouquet of sunflowers when she opens it.

"These are gorgeous, Beck. Sunflowers are my favorite."

"I can see that. Their brightness matches your energy."

"You're a romantic, huh?"

Dulce smiles and places her hand on my chest. The heat level could have convinced me that her touch had started a fire. She looks down at her hand and then back up into my eyes.

"I'd like to kiss you, would that be OK?" my voice comes out in a hoarse whisper.

"I've been waiting for you to."

I cup her chin and gently pull her toward my lips, so she ends up on her tiptoes. I lower my face to hers, breathing in her scent of honeysuckle. Our lips lightly touch and I open my mouth to taste her. Cherry lip balm flavors her lips. I am enraptured by her taste, smell, and softness.

We part, and she nuzzles her nose into my beard.

"That," I clear my throat, "was a kiss."

"You're damn right it was," Dulce responds, breathless.

5

Dulce

Our date is hilariously wonderful. A man has never made me laugh the way Beck does. His comfortableness with himself is refreshing. He does not come off cocky but self-assured. He is also very forthcoming about how he feels about me. Words like enamored, smitten, head over heels are used.

Absolute swoon.

At my front door, he kisses me goodnight. Beck has a commission to finish tomorrow but tells me he'll come down Wednesday by noon to help with the bakery. I tell him it's unnecessary, but I admit I really appreciate the extra help.

"See you on Wednesday, sweetness."

Tuesday, I build my bistro table sets. The black and white will pop in the sit down section of the bakery, next to the bright colors I plan to paint on the walls.

That evening, Beck texts me a hello and says that he was on the final finishing touches for his commission. I wish him luck and cuddle up with Moxie to watch a cooking show. Sean and I video chat a bit as well. I do manage to set up my futon before passing out tonight.

I start Wednesday off by working in the backroom. I have the glass cases to set up plus some shelving in the kitchen, but I will wait for my strong mountain man to help me. I catch myself doodling hearts on my inventory. Oops.

At noon, I peek out the door to greet Beck, but I don't see him yet. I decide I can unpack some of my pots and pans that will go in the cupboards. My A/C is struggling in the kitchen and I feel overheated. I push through with the pots, but when I pause to drink water, I notice it is 2:00 pm.

What the hell? What is up with this guy? Maybe I am fooling myself about this connection I have felt with him. I feel hurt, which I tell myself is silly since I have just met this man.

But I am hurt, and it sucks. It reminds me why I stayed single these last several years. Relationships always end up in pain. Ugh, dammit.

I wipe the sweat from my face and admit to myself I need someone to check the air conditioning unit out. I grab my purse to head over to the apartment when Beck walks through the door.

"Dude, hey thanks, but no thanks. I'm too old for games."

I sigh at his puppy dog eyes. Why does he have to be so fricken handsome?

"I am so damn sorry, Dulce. I got wrapped up in that piece from Sunday again."

"Whatever. Beck. You are a grown man. Buy an alarm clock, for frick's sake."

"You're right. I…"

"No, seriously, I'm done. I have too much going on to also juggle a guy who can't bother showing up when he says he will."

Beck nods, looking down at the floor with shame.

"You deserve everything, Dulce."

"You're good with words, but you keep failing with actions. Anyway, I need to hunt down an air conditioning repair place and continue my work day. Bye, Beck."

He stands in the doorway, staring at me. Beck slowly nods at my words, turns on his heel, and heads out the door.

That evening, after my third shower of the day, I snuggle with Moxie and watch more cooking shows. Cooking shows are like comfort food to me. They also give me ideas about unique flavor combinations, which is one of my specialties.

A knock at the door wakes me up from my television stupor.

"Who is it?" I call out. It's close to 9:00.

"Beck. I'm sorry it's so late, but I have something for you."

I look down at my clothes. I'm wearing my Smurfs nightie and kitten slippers. I shrug my shoulders - it's not like he and I are even happening here.

I open the door and find Beck wearing the same clothing as earlier but covered in more paint.

"May I come in? I won't be long. I just wanted to give this to you."

I shrug and let him inside.

"I am sorry I was late. There is no excuse. It was wrong. This is the piece I got so wrapped up in and I want you to have it."

Beck turns the canvas around. The painting he shows me is full of vibrant color. I can feel the warmth radiating off the picture. Amongst the ocean waves, a beautiful woman is turning into a swan on the canvas. The progression reminds me of the phases of the moon. I bend down to look closer and softly gasp.

"Is that, is that me?"

"Yes, sweetness. You inspired me by sharing your beautiful, true self with me on the night of the wedding that I had to paint you."

I feel my eyes well up. Whatever anger I felt drifted away. I still feel cautious in the back of my mind, but I choose to go with my heart. I reach over the painting and touch Beck's scruffy cheek.

"Thank you. That is the most beautiful thing anyone has ever given me."

Next thing I know, the painting is resting on my kitchen table and Beck is scooping me up into his arms. He carries me to the futon where Moxie makes an annoyed greeting and scrambles away. Beck laughs.

"I can see she's going to make me work for her approval."

I kiss him long and deep. His beard feels good against my skin, a roughness that makes me wet.

Beck slides me back and lifts up my nightie.

"I know you have an early morning, so do I," he says.

My nightie is pushed up to my breasts, and he kisses my belly.

"I just want to help set you up for a good night's sleep. May I?"

My heart races and I take a slow, deep breath before I can respond.

"A goodnight's sleep sounds amazing."

As soon as I say this, Beck slides his hands behind me, gripping my ass cheeks. The squeeze feels good and my pussy throbs. He kisses my inner thighs with his rough face. I look down and I see my inner thighs turning bright pink from his beard. Beck looks up at me and smiles while he slides a finger inside. I groan and throw my head back. He adds another finger and pumps in and out. I feel myself grow more and more slick as he fingerfucks me.

"You like that?" he asks with a gravelly voice.

"Yes," I breathe out, "Don't stop."

I then feel his tongue find my clit while he continues to pump me hard. Curse words escape my mouth as I grab a handful of his long, copper brown hair in ecstasy. Beck does not have to suck my clit for long. My entire body explodes into an orgasm. Both of my

The Mountain Merman's Love Connection

hands are on his head now, gripping his hair as I come. Moxie meows a complaint from under the futon.

Beck crawls up to me, nuzzles into my neck, and stands up. This absolute hottie then tucks me in. I snuggle into my quilt and stare up at my gorgeous mountain man.

"I'll call you tomorrow."

He kisses me goodbye and heads out the door.

6

Dulce

The last four weeks in Branwen Beach have been a whirlwind. Because of the air conditioning problem and lack of HVAC repair shops, I was forced to delay my grand opening by a couple of weeks. Beck came to the rescue, though, with two of his high school mates, Aiden and Tyson, who work on the other side of the mountain in Corvid Valley. He paid for their hotel room while they stayed in town to fix my air conditioning.

The week before my grand opening, Beck offers to paint a mural on an inside wall of the bakery. He tells me he put his work commissions on hold for the week so he can focus on helping me. Whatever I need.

I know what I want. I want this man in my bed as of yesterday. We have spent many nights together at this point, but he has always insisted on focusing only on my pleasure.

"I promise I want you. I just want to feel like I've earned you, after being such a flake," he whispered into my ear last night as he fucked me with my favorite vibrator. Then he dove for my dark nipple, sucking my entire breast into his mouth.

Now I stand in front of my bakery, watching Beck install the sign above my front door. I went with something simple,

Branwen Beach Bakery. The swirly font compliments the whimsy of Paige's storefront.

"How does it look?"

"Perfect. You nailed it on the first try."

"Alright, my sweetness, I am coming down and it's now time to present you with the mural."

Beck only worked on the mural when I retired for the day to my apartment or ran errands. Otherwise, he kept it well hidden behind a painter's tarp.

"OK, big guy, show me your baby."

I grab his hand and squeeze it.

Beck sweeps the tarp down and before me is a cheerful beach scene with tourists enjoying themselves and surfable waves in the background. I scan the painting, there are so many details to discover, and see on the left side that there's a small beach cave. Inside the cave is a merman and a swan snuggling together.

"I love this. You put so much thought into this."

Yet again, I was welling up. I'm a sucker for romantic gestures. Beck pulls me close to him and kisses me.

"I'm glad you like it," he brushes a stray hair out of my face. "Now I'm going to head home so you can have time at your place. Tomorrow is a big day for you."

I hug him close to me and say, "Thank you for helping me get to this point. I really appreciate all the time you've given me to reach my dream."

Beck grins and points to his new smart watch.

"Best purchase of my life, I think."

Monday is a whirlwind of powdered sugar, cash register beeps, and flakey pastry. The morning starts off with a line out the door. I was mistaken when I didn't hire help. I wanted to see how the first week or two went. Paige is a lifesaver, though, and sends her employee, Rex, over to help me during the breakfast and lunch rushes.

Three in the afternoon rolls around and I flip on the closed sign. My cleaning crew will come tonight, so I stack the chairs, wipe down the surfaces, and lug the trash out to the dumpster. I glimpse myself in the mirror by the back door.

My apron is covered in flour, which is also speckled on my face. The hair wrapped in my bun has mutinied. Auburn and gray strands are flying every which way. I laugh at myself and reach for the strands when I hear the bell above the door twinkle. I forgot to lock the front.

Beck stands in the doorway, holding a bottle of wine.

"You're a sight for sore eyes," I say, surprised. We had made no plans.

"Are you finished up here? I have a bagful of groceries in my car plus a bottle of bubble bath. Time for the professional baker to end her first day in style."

I sit across from Beck, wrapped in my terry-cloth robe, fed and smelling of lavender bath water.

"Why don't I tuck in my girl before I head out?"

"I'd like for you to stay, if you can?"

"Really? You're not ready to pass out?"

"Oh, I'm ready. But I've been dying to feel you inside me for weeks now. I can't think of a better way to end this fabulous day."

Beck stands up and walks over to my side of the kitchen table. He twirls my wet hair then fists it at the nape of my neck.

"Are you asking me to fuck you, sweetness?"

"Yes, please," I breathe out, my pussy immediately becoming a throbbing, hot mound.

Beck lifts me to standing like I weigh nothing. He sweeps me off my feet and lays me down on the flattened futon. My robe opens, and he lightly travels his fingertips along my skin. When he reaches my nipples, he teases them with a soft touch until he gives the left one a good pinch. I moan out and jut my hips toward him. He cups their sides and pulls me closer to him.

Leaning down between my thighs, Beck looks up at me.

"Give me this pussy. It's mine."

I lift my hips up so that my wetness is in front of his mouth. He licks my swollen lips as I moan loudly. Beck's tongue travels to my inner thighs, where he playfully licks and bites me.

"I need you in me. Come here."

Beck crawls up to me, licking my nipples as he travels. We become eye level, and I feel the head of his cock teasing my pussy.

"You're awfully wet, sweetness. Were you hoping for this?"

Beck pushes his head in, then slides it out. I groan out in frustration and open my legs further to encourage him.

We kiss and breathe heavily while teasing each other.

"Fuck me with that thick cock."

"This one?" Beck rubs his shaft on my throbbing clit.

"Yes. Own my pussy," I groan out the last word as he enters me.

Beck pins my arms above my head while he bends down to lick my tits. I am not long for this world. The orgasm is boiling up in me.

"Harder. I'm going to come on your cock."

Beck roughly fucks me as I climax, and once I peak, he comes as well. We lay there, his throbbing, spent member resting inside of me.

I must have fallen asleep because the next thing I know, he's getting me up to brush my teeth.

We crawl into bed together, and I curl up in his arms. My head rests on his chest. I drift off to sleep, feeling the rise and fall of his chiseled pecs.

7

Beck

I wake up in Dulce's bed with the morning light dancing on my face.

"Hey sleepyhead, coffee?"

The smell of hazelnut coffee meets my nose. I sit up, catching her eyes lingering on my chest. Her eyes meet mine and she blushes.

"Like what you see, sweetness?" I say, winking at her.

"You damn well know I do," Dulce laughs, but then her face turns serious.

"What's up?" I don't hide the worry in my voice.

Dulce stands up and paces.

"Beck, what we have found with each other is amazing. I have fallen hard, big time."

"Well, that doesn't sound so bad to me? I know you're the woman for me."

Dulce stops pacing and gives me a look that gives me butterflies. What I wouldn't do to make this woman my wife.

"I'm just going to spit it out. I don't want to move onto the mountain. I love you, but I need to stay in town with my business, especially these fledgling years."

"Who said anything about moving to the mountain?"

I apparently said the wrong thing because Dulce's face falls.

"Oh wow, I feel like such an idiot," she laughs derisively, "I crazy jumped the gun. Of course. This is all still so new, you're not even close to considering something serious."

Her voice cracks and I bound out of bed, wrapping my arms around her. Dulce tucks into me flawlessly. She is a perfect fit.

"Sweetness, of course, I see this as something serious. I see this as something forever."

Dulce looks up at me with a red nose and stuffily asks, "You do?"

"Hell yes I do. And I figured we would live down here because of the bakery. Nevermind I can't see a spirit like yours happy in constant solitude. I can work anywhere."

Dulce squeals and jumps on me. She wraps her legs around my waist and kisses every inch of my face.

"I love you, Beck. So damn much."

Dulce's gloved hand holds mine as we walk on the beach. The sun is setting earlier on these chilly October nights and we take advantage of the ocean views every chance we get. Our walk is intimate in its silence until Dulce lets out a "huh!"

"You OK?"

"Yeah, I was just realizing that this is the spot where your brother and Paige were married."

"I think you're right."

I smile down at her.

"Why do you look like the cat who ate the canary?"

"Well, my sweetness, I led us in this direction on purpose. This is the spot where our eyes first met."

As I say this, I go down on one knee. Dulce's hands fly up to her gaping mouth. I retrieve the ring box from my back pocket and flip it open.

"Dulce, my sweetness, I have never met a woman like you. You are radiant, persistent, brave, vibrant, an absolute knockout. Will you do the honor of becoming my wife?"

"Yes!" she screams against the crashing waves, tackling me onto the sand. We roll around, laughing and kissing.

Epilogue

Dulce

"Happy Valentine's Day, sweetness."

Beck hands me a mug of tea. Outside the cabin, the wind howls and the snow dances on our window. We cuddle under a throw blanket in front of the fire.

"Our weekend getaway may turn into a long weekend getaway," I say, watching the snow swirl.

"I can't think of anyone else I'd rather be snowed in with than my sexy wife."

I snuggle into him.

"I'm glad Liora can cover for me at the bakery. She's been so helpful. You know she may start selling her bread as a side hustle?"

"She will make bank. Her bread is the shit."

"She should totally use that as her tagline," I giggle.

I stand up to use the bathroom for the hundredth time today. This has been an issue for about a week and I am wondering if I have a UTI.

The medicine cabinet is partially open when I walk in. I reach to close it and notice the pregnancy test kit I bought a couple of months ago during our last cabin weekend. My delayed period started before I used it, so I just tucked it away.

Testing can't hurt. We haven't been trying, but it's not like we have been preventing, either. I am a few days late, but I also don't have a regular cycle.

The plus sign blazes from the test stick in less than five minutes. I walk out into the living room and find Beck snoring on the couch. I resist waking him and crawl under the blanket to wait, but he wakes up to my soft jostling.

"Hey there," Beck nuzzles into my neck.

"I have some news, babe."

I hold up the pregnancy test stick. Beck's green eyes widen as he looks between the test stick and me. He pulls me close and kisses me hard.

"Dulce Atwater, I am so incredibly happy. I love you, sweetness."

"I love you too, future pops."

A MOUNTAIN
MERMAN
ROMANCE

THE MOUNTAIN MERMAN'S *First Kiss*

KAT VROMAN

1

CARLOW

"Listen, I get it, you are a cave-dwelling hermit, but I need you to have found a wife as of yesterday."

My older brother Murphy stands in my kitchen with a beer in hand, appearing ready to fall on his knees and beg profusely at my feet.

"You are literally standing in my two-bedroom house. I'll begrudgingly accept hermit, but this ain't no cave."

My comment makes my two other older brothers, Beck and Lachlan, laugh and shake their heads.

Beck slaps Murphy on the back and sits down next to me.

"Murphy, bro, give the family baby some slack. Madame Liora is on the case and even she hasn't found someone for him yet."

"I get that, but it's been well over a year since I hired her. Lachlan here just had his one-year anniversary. Beck is married with a baby arriving next month, for fricks sake. The king is getting impatient, which is making me impatient."

"I'm sorry your father-in-law is on you about this, but I think Liora hasn't found me a match yet because I just don't have a true love mate out there. That's why I have never dated," I say with a shrug. "I have never met someone who has made me feel like rubbing all up against them."

All three brothers laugh at me, and Beck puts his arm around my shoulders.

"I promise, there's more to it than that."

"OK, whatever. I just don't see it happening. If the King won't get off your back, maybe in a year or so I'll be willing to have an arranged marriage. But that sounds like hell, so I'd like to put it off for as long as possible."

"I don't want you to be unhappy, little brother. I have faith that Madame Liora will match you with someone you will truly love. I just wish it was happening faster. My father-in-law is going to have to chill out. I know there's someone out there who will find your merman butt adorable. "

Lachlan claps his hands together loudly and announces, "OK, we need to move on. We didn't meet here to discuss Carlow's love life."

My sister-in-law, Princess Mair, is a philanthropist and runs a thriving charity. After the success of her Paranormal Orphanage and Academy on Ravenhart Mountain, she has tasked us to create a wellness lodge up here as well. Mair's goal is to make it the Ronald McDonald House for adults with activities such as equestrian therapy and yoga. I will design the furniture, although my wood shop is too small to produce what we will need.

"Carlow, let's meet at some point to discuss the aesthetic so that we're aligned with your furniture and my art pieces," Beck, the professional artist of the family, offers.

"Sounds good. Murphy, does Mair have any specific ideas or is she OK with us to present our own?

"The only thing she said is that she wants everything tied in with the mountain woods and nature."

After a two-hour brainstorming session, my brothers head out the door. Murphy is the last to leave and reminds me of our cousin's engagement party in a few days. He closes the door behind him.

Ugh, I hate parties.

I look around at the mess, sigh, and start cleaning. I won't be able to relax here and unwind until the clutter from my brothers' visit is gone.

The September evenings are becoming cooler. I open up my flue and build my first fire of the season. The living room fills with the smell of wood burning. I make a mug of hot cocoa and set myself up on my plush leather reading chair. I love my brothers, but their visits require a good amount of recovery time for me. Although, I would choose them over dealing with strangers any day of the week.

I am 5 chapters into my new book when my cell rings.

"Madame Liora? This is unexpected. How are you?"

"Happy National Cream-Filled Donut evening, Carlow!"

"Uh, yes, happy donut day to you as well?"

Per usual, I sound awkward.

"So, Carlow, I am about to have surgery and won't be able to bake for a bit. Since it's been a while since your last order, I was wondering if you would like a bread basket this week before I pause the business during my healing process?"

I apparently am holding my breath, listening to her, and slowly let out a lungful of air. Relief washes over me when I realize she is calling about her delicious bread and not some woman I will have to meet.

"Of course! I do love your bread."

"Wonderful!"

2

Fernanda

I powder my pink, swollen nose for the 100th time.

Shit.

It's still very obvious that I have been crying. I am late to the book club and my arrival will not go unnoticed.

Fernanda Ramos, get your head in the game. You should have left Cody months ago. He was not a kind boyfriend. You may be "too much" for him, but there is someone out there who you are just the right amount of Fernanda for.

The sob I am holding in during my pep talk to myself escapes and the tears break free from their prison yet again.

What-the-fuck-ever, I am just going to head over to Liora's now. Maybe my patchy red tomato face will transform on the drive.

I enter Liora's backyard to see my fellow book club ladies enjoying mimosas. Paige and Zora wave in my direction. The early afternoon sun is warm enough for the outdoor book club, but I have a feeling next time we will meet inside.

Liora sweeps around the corner holding an enormous platter of pastries and announces, "Happy National Cream-Filled Donut Day, lay—"

She stops, dead in her tracks, spotting me at the patio door. Liora's expression tells me everything I need to know - she knows I've been a blubbering mess.

"Fern! Come with me, my darling."

Liora hands the tray to Paige and rushes over to me, ushering me back into the house.

"Oh Liora, I don't want to make a scene. I don't want to interrupt the book club meeting."

"Pish posh, those ladies haven't even started. My famous mimosas and donuts will keep them busy for now. Sit, sit."

Liora plops down on her couch and pats the cushion next to her.

"You've always been so kind to me, Liora. It's nothing big, just another break up. I sure know how to pick men."

I laugh derisively while sniffing.

"That Cody fellow? He did have a sour disposition to him."

My voice cracks as I wail out, "He said I was too much for him. I am a lot. I'm always a lot. I don't think I am meant to be a girlfriend. These men always tire of me. Me just being me."

Liora hands me a tissue and puts her arm around my shoulders.

"Now listen here, young lady."

"I'm 41," I choke out. "The Young Lady Ship has sailed for me."

"Well, that's just bunk! You have plenty of life left to live, Fern Ramos. Look at me, missy."

Liora grasps my hands to get me to look up at her.

"Oh!" she exclaims.

"You OK?"

"I sure am," Liora says as she stands up and begins to pace the room.

"Fern, did you know I am having surgery in a couple of days?"

"I remember you said that was a possibility. How can I help? Do you have a ride?"

"Yes, Ev is helping me out for the week. But now that you mention it, I will have an order for a customer up on the mountain that I won't be able to deliver during my recovery. Could you help an old woman out?"

"Of course," I wipe my eyes, "Is that why you reacted like that?"

"Sorry, it just popped into my head then. Thank you, my dear. Ev or I will let you know when to pick the delivery. Now, come here for a hug. I think you need a mimosa, a donut, and some book club smut talk."

A couple of days later, Ev calls me to let me know Liora's

surgery went well and that the bread order is ready for me to pick up.

"I don't get off from the hotel until 3:00. Is that OK? How far is this person's place up the mountain?"

"It's about an hour. So you should be able to drop it off and head back down before dark. Thank you so much. Liora was very excited about you helping with this delivery."

I hang up, thinking about how that was an odd statement. But, Liora is an odd lady. A fun, hilarious, wise but odd lady. And single, from what I can tell. Maybe that's my future, being the local whacky old lady in town.

After work, I head straight to Dulce's bakery, which is where Liora works out of for her bread baking side business. Dulce is waiting for me with a big smile.

"You're awfully happy today. I take it that the pregnancy is going well?"

She laughs and rubs her rotund belly.

"Today has been fine, but morning sickness still plagues me.
"

She points to a couple of boxes on a table.

"The address is taped to the order. You're such a sweetie for doing this for Madame Liora."

"She's such a cool lady. I am happy to help."

I drive up the mountain in my beat up Civic with the windows down. The mountain air is crisp, causing me to have a sudden craving for hot apple cider. The leaves are changing and I spy flashes of orange and gold along my drive.

My GPS instructs me to take a right along a windy, long driveway. At the end of it stands a two-story log cabin. It is gorgeous. I spot a lake in the background as well. I am not sure which lake this is since Ravenhart Mountain boasts several.

I hop out of the car and start getting the delivery ready when I hear the front door open. I look up to see a beast of a man, standing maybe 6'4", with chestnut hair and a close-cut beard. His flannel shirt has a few buttons open and wisps of chest hair peek out. Our eyes meet and my pussy switch flips to on.

Holy Good Looking, Batman.

3

Carlow

The most beautiful woman I have ever seen is standing in my driveway. Her hair is the color of dark walnut and it falls in waves, stopping right above her voluptuous chest. I watch her walk toward me; her round hips swaying back and forth. She now stands before me and her mouth is moving, but all I hear is the color of her espresso eyes.

"Sir?"

"Oh, sorry. I was lost in thought. Are you the delivery girl?"

"Girl?"

The woman laughs at me. Because why not?

"I don't think I have been referred to as a girl for many moons. But, yes, I have Liora's baking order for you. Do you mind helping me? We can do it in one trip together."

I think I say yes to her, but my head is now filled with anxious bees as I walk beside this stunning woman. Her shirt's scoop neck plunges just enough for me to see her cleavage staring up at me. I feel myself harden as she hands me a box. Can she tell? This is why I am a hermit, like Murphy said. I don't know how to behave around other people. I lead the way back to my home, feeling my cheeks burn with embarrassment and desire.

I show this woman to my kitchen and quickly get behind the island to hide my bulge. She opens the boxes to review my order, but all I can hear is buzzzzzz and I'm lost in the scent of peaches. Brushing by me to open the box I brought in and I realize it's her hair that smells like peaches. She is smiling expectantly at me, and I snap out of my delirium.

"Uh, thank you for bringing these."

"Of course! I'm Fernanda, by the way, but most folks call me Fern."

Fernanda, the Dark Walnut Goddess, reaches out her hand for me to shake. It hovers right over my pulsating thickness, but she's looking straight into my eyes and does not notice.

"I'm Carlow. Thank you, drive safe."

I shake her hand, but her face falls a bit after I speak.

"Well, enjoy."

I watch the most perfect woman walk out of my home, closing the door behind her. I stand there, staring at the door, wondering what the hell just happened. The scent of peaches lingers in the air. I fight the urge to run after her. I don't know what I would say or do, but I want to stop her from leaving.

I walk to the door, grumble a bit, then walk back to the kitchen island. I repeat this nonsense several times. On my fourth go around. When I reach the door, I fling it open. I expect to see an empty driveway. Instead, I see Fernanda, the Goddess with Espresso Eyes, walking back up my front steps.

"Oh!"

I have startled her with my dramatic-because-I-am-a-freak door opening.

"Sorry, the door got away from me. Did you forget something?"

"My car isn't starting."

"I can take a look, I guess."

Why did I just offer to do that? I don't know crap about cars. I'm a furniture builder. Look at me here, walking to her car, and asking her to pop the hood. I have entered the Upside

Down and I don't know how to return to my plane of existence.

I come up with the manly suggestion to give her car a jump start, but that ends up being a bust. By now, the sun is setting behind the trees. Fern is looking at her phone for a rideshare, shivering in the crisp evening air.

"Damn, there's nothing."

"Come inside. I'll start a fire. It's too cold out here to stand around."

Inside, I put on the teakettle and get a fire started. I fish a wool throw blanket out of my trunk for Fern to warm up under. Then I call Lachlan, who lives about a half hour below me on the mountain.

"Hey little brother, what's up?"

"Hey, if a car won't start and a jump start fails, it's probably the alternator, right?"

"Yup. Your Jeep OK? I thought we just replaced your alternator last spring?"

"We did. This is for a friend of Liora's. Her car died in my driveway. Think you could help her?"

"A friend of Madame Liora's?"

I hear my sister-in-law, Paige, in the background, make a little shriek.

"Of course I will help her. But it'll have to wait until the morning when there's light and I can get her a new one in town. Text me the info about her type of car, OK?" my brother says.

"Got it. Thanks."

I hang up and look over at the beauty sitting on my couch. Right then, the kettle whistles. I pour us each a cup of boiling water and bring a few tea bag options over to Fern.

"Wow, it's like I'm at some nice B&B. The chamomile would be great, thank you."

"My brother will be here in the morning to fix your car. I have a guest bedroom upstairs that is all yours. Have you eaten?"

I feel like a dork because I am proud that I managed to invite her over without breaking into hives. She thanks me profusely and offers to help cook.

Fern peeks into my fridge and suggests we make pasta with her gourmet meat sauce. We chat in the kitchen while we get the meal together. Well, she chats. And she asks questions. I answer. I'm not that rude. But I am finding it increasingly difficult to maintain any sort of conversation with her. Talking with someone I don't know well always zaps my strength, but I am also enamored by this woman. Fern is not only breathtaking, but she's a ball of quirky, yet charming, energy. I love it, but it's also overwhelming for me.

The meal is incredible. I don't know what she put in that sauce but I may have convinced her to sell it as a side hustle. She laughs at the suggestion, then gets quiet.

"Sorry, did I say something wrong?"

"No, no, not at all. I was just thinking how nice it is to break bread with a man who says supportive, kind things to me."

Fernanda's dark eyes focus on my own and I feel my insides turn into butterscotch pudding.

"Oh?"

"Sorry, I just had a bad relationship end. I won't bore you. Thank you for the sweet words. I appreciate them. Anyway, I'll help you clean up and head to bed so that I am out of your hair."

"Please, no, you're my guest. I'll clean up. Let me first get you linens and show you your room."

We stand up together. She is inches away and smiling up at me. I have never had the urge to kiss a woman, or anyone, until right at this moment. I turn around abruptly and whack my thigh on the table.

"You OK?" Fern asks with worry in her voice.

"Just a klutz," I say, knowing full well I am blushing beneath my beard.

As much as I want to soak her in, I know my limits. This woman needs to hole up in the guest room now, for my own sanity.

4

CARLOW

Fern and I sit quietly, reading the mountain newspaper, while drinking coffee and enjoying toast from one of Liora's loaves. A rap on the door breaks the silence.

Lachlan pokes his head through the front door.

"Fern, your car is all set. Carlow, I got to run. A client is getting itchy."

"Thank you so much! How much do I owe you?"

"It's on the house. I hope to see you again, Fern. Maybe at a family event or something."

Lachlan winks at me and leaves.

"Family event?"

"Oh, who knows? My older brother likes to cause trouble."

"Oh, OK."

Fern takes a sip of her coffee with disappointed eyes.

Quick, make Fern the Quirky Charming Goddess smile.

"It's no big deal, really. My cousin Chet's engagement party is tomorrow night. Lachlan was just being silly. I'm sure you wouldn't want to go to something like that."

"Well, would you like me to go to something like that?"

I may have just turned blind. I think the shock of her question caused me to factory reset. I try to form words, but nothing happens. Then, a second later, I blurt out one sentence at the speed of light.

"I would absolutely love for you to go to something like that."

Fern's eyes go wide at my roadrunner mouth, but then she smiles.

"OK, I'm in."

***

Chet and Vanna's party is at my auntie's house. Per usual, Auntie Luann went 110% over the top. Guests, ice sculptures, and two chocolate fountains fill her home to overflowing. I want to crawl out of my skin, but Fern looks like she is enjoying herself, so I don't want to make her leave early.

Several guests clink their glasses with silverware. Fern takes my hand, which may fall off now because of the electric heat that ran up my arm, and guides me to the back of the room. We can still hear the speakers, but the air is cooler and I am grateful she brought me to a more open area. When she leans in to me, her peach scent envelopes my senses until her whisper breaks through.

"I think you're safe to bail after this last speech."

Right then, several party goers exclaim while staring out the window into the night. Huge flakes of snow are falling. Crap, this storm was supposed to miss the mountain.

"We better go. The road will be closed soon," I say.

Fern and I drive back to my place slowly. When we arrive, we find her car half covered in snow.

"OK, I realize this is wonky because we didn't even know each other a week ago, but I am going to have to insist you're my guest again. It's much too dangerous to drive right now."

Fern beams up at me.

"My very own B&B again."

Inside, I start the fire and make us tea. Fern peruses my bookshelf and picks out an Agatha Christie.

"Hey, I could tell tonight was a lot for you."

I shuffle awkwardly and Fern continues.

"It's fine. It was a lot. I couldn't even tell what the difference was between those two chocolate fountains."

I laugh. I still feel awkward interacting with her, but she seems to roll with it.

"Anyway, I was going to suggest we just chill the rest of the night. If it's OK with you, I haven't read this Agatha Christie book before. Is it cool that I read in front of the fire? It's so cozy with the snow falling outside."

"I'd love that."

My voice sounds soft, and I take a pause, thinking that I sound pathetic, but Fern is grinning at me from ear to ear. I get over myself, grab the biography I'm reading, and settle onto the couch.

The evening meanders along. Outside, the wind is picking up, adding a howling sound in my chimney. Fern and I stay wrapped up in our throw blankets, reading, sipping tea, staring at the fire, and smiling at each other from time to time. I cannot remember the last time I felt this content with a person. With the various cats I have adopted through the years, for sure. But this may be the first time I am at this level of peace with another person. I did not want the feeling to end.

5

Fernanda

I sit in my office shredding a boxful of documents I could have given my assistant. But I need this meditative activity at the moment. It's been several days since I left Carlow's cabin on that frosty morning, and I have not heard a peep from him.

At first, I didn't mind because I told myself I did not want a dating life that involved driving a two hour round trip up and down a mountain. Then I told myself that he clearly doesn't like me. But even that lie didn't stick for long. I know he likes me. After our first evening together, I knew I could read him like a book. It was something in his blue eyes.

I've never experienced that before.

Now, here I am, creating my own snow with paper. It doesn't feel right not seeking him out one more time. We need to talk. I doubt he likes confrontation, but I'm already walking out my office door with my keys and coat, so anyway…

The Mountain Merman's First Kiss

I first stop at Liora's since I had texted earlier that I would pop by today to check in on her. I am surprised to find her and Ev in the kitchen, baking up a big mess.

"Liora? Are you supposed to be doing this?"

I'm such a nanny dog.

"Doc gave me the OK this morning. I can bake but I can't lift anything still. Speaking of, Fern dear, I forgot to include my crispy breadsticks in Carlow's order. Will you do me one more favor and be a doll and deliver this box to him?"

Liora motions to a box sitting on the kitchen table. I give her a quick hug, grab the box, and head to my car.

I drive with the windows down again and allow the smell of future rain to clear my head. I don't know what to expect from Carlow, but I know I need to at least speak with him.

I find him outside, setting up a rocking chair on his porch.

"Is that a Carlow creation?"

My shy mountain man stands up with a start, but then fixes his sexy smile onto me.

"I didn't know you were coming over. Yeah, just made this piece. What do you think?"

I walk up, hand him the breadsticks, and then brush by him to sit down on the rocker. Heat radiates from our bodies when we're so close. It almost feels like an energy current. I noticed it at the engagement party as well.

I sit down and slowly rock, staring up at his tall frame, knowing perfectly well he can see right down my shirt.

"I love it."

He gives his sexy grin again, plus I can see that he is blushing underneath his graying beard. I stand up, our faces an inch away from each other. I open my mouth to speak, but he steps back, a sudden look of discomfort on his handsome face.

"Carlow, before I go, I think we should talk."

He nods toward me but is deeply interested in the porch post.

"OK, I'm just going to cut to the chase. I have feelings for you, Carlow. I can't stop thinking about you. And I want to know if you feel the same way."

I believe this to be the first time I've ever watched a man turn pale to puke green back to pale in front of my eyes. Carlow clears his throat twice before grunting out a "yes."

My heart attempts to break free from my chest while my thrumming pussy soaks my panties. I step toward Carlow and place my hand on his defined chest. He jumps back, his eyes a mixture of heat and fear.

"I can't. You don't know. I've never had a girlfriend. I have never even kissed a woman. I can't believe I have to tell you this. It is so embarrassing. You deserve so, so much more than what I can offer."

I close my mouth as soon as I notice it's open, but he already sees my reaction. I don't know what I expected, but the hottest man on earth being a virgin was not it.

Carlow clears his throat and blurts out, "And I am also a merman. I get that it's weird and creepy for a human. I'm a merman."

He shrugs his shoulders as if what he said is the final deciding factor.

"Yeah, no kidding. I was at Paige and Lachlan's wedding."

"Oh. Well, my point still stands."

"I came here because I like you. I like you as a merman. I didn't know you any other way. And we can figure the rest out."

Carlow shakes his head, his hands twisting around each other.

"No, Fern, I'm sorry. I need to be alone now. Please go."

The Mountain Merman's First Kiss

Without another word, I spin on my heel and go down the steps. I count quietly to myself as I walk to my car. I breathe and count while I open the door. Two more breaths as I buckle up. Backing up requires counting with rough breaths every couple of numbers.

I finally am on the road, and the tears come. I pull off into a turnout and feel the feels.

6

Carlow

I hear the car's engine fade.

I don't know what the hell is happening. The world's most perfect woman just confessed her feelings for me, and I verbally vomited all over her. I told Fern my deepest shame - that I'm too much of a freak for a woman to love me.

And she didn't reject me.

I rejected her. Now I feel like puking everywhere and giving myself a high five because I made the right choice.

I head to the lake, strip, and plunge into the cold water. Soon I am beating my tail to speed myself up. I swim as fast as I can to the other side of the lake and back. My anxiety courses through my veins, so I repeatedly swim back and forth across the lake until it mostly subsides.

Took me 46 round trips and two hours of my day.

On the lakeshore, I pull on my jeans and notice I have several missed calls from Lachlan.

"Hey, is everything OK? I see you called a bunch."

"Why the hell is Paige's book club friend in my house crying to her over you?"

"Huh? What book club friend?"

"Fern, dummy. The one whose car I fixed."

"Fern is in a book club with Paige?"

"Holy shit, dude, you are acting really clueless."

I hear him open his screen door, followed by early evening crickets in the background. Lachlan continues in a hushed voice.

"Do you have feelings for this woman?"

"I do, but that's not the point. Fernanda is such an amazing woman. She deserves someone who is experienced in relationships, not some weirdo like me."

My brother sighs.

"Let's take this one step at a time. How did you meet Fern?"

"She delivered my bakery order because she offered to help Liora during her surgery recovery."

"You don't say."

I don't appreciate my brother's mocking tone, but I don't interrupt him.

"Little brother, Beck and I have been helping Liora with all of her orders since her surgery. She did not need Fern to do shit."

"Oh, then why..."

"Seriously dude, stop and think," my brother interrupts me.

I stare out at the lake, my head threatening to explode with a sudden realization. Lachlan is right. I am a dummy.

"Dude, I need to go. I need to think."

I run into the house to grab my jacket and keys. I need some time to think, but I can do that on the drive.

And, boy, do I think. I had not even considered that Liora had sent Fern to me on purpose. I was so overwhelmed by my reaction to her I didn't take a minute to stop and think about why I was reacting so strongly to her presence. I chose to close myself off again. I got in my way again.

I smack my steering wheel and yell, "I'm sick of this crap!"

I have never felt so determined in my life. The closest to this was when I realized how much I loved furniture making. This is much more intense, however.

Branwen Beach is quiet this evening. The summer tourists are long gone and the autumn stillness has set in. I pull into Lachlan's driveway and he greets me at the door.

"She left, man. Sorry, I didn't realize you were coming here."

"Do you know where she went?"

"She said she had to finish up some work tasks," called Paige from inside the house.

"Go get her, tiger!!" Lachlan shouts at me as I peel out of the driveway.

Branwen Beach Hotel's lobby is dimly lit. A young woman greets me and goes into the back when I ask about Fernanda. Fern comes out of the lobby with a surprised look in her red eyes.

"What are you doing here?"

"I'd like to talk to you. And apologize. Definitely apologize."

"Uh, OK. Sandra, keep an eye on things. Carlow, you can come back in here."

I follow her into the back office. Fern turns to me and my verbal vomit unleashes itself once again.

"I have spent my life avoiding most people and situations I don't feel fully in control of. Which was fine for many years, but then I met you. Before you, not one woman turned my head. Hell, not one man, either. I figured I wasn't made that way, the way that most people seem to be made. I wasn't on this planet to fall in love or be loved romantically, at least. So I found my passion for furniture making and living a peaceful life up on the mountain.

"I thought I loved my life. But then you show up in my driveway and my entire worldview spun out of control and into the lake. I acted just as bonkers as I felt. You were the victim of my foolishness, and I am sorry. I totally realize you probably want nothing to do with me now that you know I'm an anxious mess of a virgin, but I had to give it one last shot. I'm in love with you, Fernanda."

My heart races and I breathe in slowly, staring at the carpet. A peach scent drifts past my nose. I look up to find Fern standing an inch away from me, gently touching my arm.

The Mountain Merman's First Kiss

"You hungry? I haven't eaten yet and there's homemade lasagna at my place. Want to join me?"

We sit on Fern's couch, full of lasagna, salad, and wine. I am not much of a drinker and drank just one glass, but I feel looser. That may also be from the high I am feeling from Fern's forgiveness.

She appeared to forgive me instantly. I'm baffled. I asked halfway through the dinner if she is sure she didn't want time to decide if I am worth the trouble.

"I don't see you as trouble at all, Carlow. I see you as the man I am in love with. And knowing you love me back makes figuring all of this out a lot less stressful."

On the couch, Fern tells her smart speaker to play her favorites. Marvin Gaye croons. I close my eyes and take a quiet breath. I want to jump up and take off. My nerves are at a boiling point. As I internally lecture myself to chill out, I feel her hand lightly touch my knee. I open my eyes to see Fern staring at me in a gentle and loving way.

"So you've never kissed anyone before?"

"No," my voice comes out strangled.

"I want to kiss you. Is that OK?"

"Yes," I breathe, gripping the couch pillow to ground myself.

Fern scoots up to me, her soft mouth brushing my own. She opens her lips slightly, allowing them to dance on mine, coaxing my mouth to open. As soon as it does, Fern lightly sucks on my lower lip, then slides her tongue into my mouth. She tastes like red wine and strawberry salad dressing. I allow my tongue to meet hers and flames shoot up from my rock hard bulge. She senses my excitement, wrapping her hand behind my neck, digging her fingers into my hair, and kissing me harder. The scent of peaches encircles me.

    I have never felt so much bliss.

7

Fernanda

I jump up and down, cheering my strike. Whipping around, I see Carlow laugh and hide his hands in his face. I saunter over to him, letting my hips sway.

"Another strike, good sir."

"How are you so good at this?"

Carlow stands up and wraps his hands around my waist. It's been a few weeks since our first kiss and he has just started making the first move this week. Baby steps.

"I love kissing you," I breathe into his ear when I hear a familiar, yet unwelcome, voice behind me.

"You've gotta be shittin' me."

We turn to see my ex, Cody, standing there with some random woman hanging off of him. He smirks in my direction, then sizes up Carlow.

"Hi Cody," I say as dryly as possible.

"Who's the dweeb?"

"Oh fuck off, Cody. Go bowl."

I turn my back to him, but he walks up to Carlow, holding out his hand.

"Hey dude, I'm this one's ex. She's a real chore," he laughs, observing Carlow's inner anxiety show up on his face, "but you seem to be a piece of work as well. Come on, babe, let's leave these losers alone."

The random girl laughs and pops her gum. I watch them walk away, turn to Carlow to say something, and discover he is gone.

Crap.

I walk around the loud bowling alley, but I do not see him. That makes sense, since I would bet money that he escaped to somewhere private. I try the men's bathroom but a gruff voice yells "OCCUPIED!" to my knock.

I search my purse for my phone but realize I had left it in the car. I beeline it to the exit, walking by Cody and his date renting shoes.

"Where's your freak boyfriend, Fernie?" he sneers.

"Go dingle your tiny mushroom at your date and fuck off, Cody."

I stomp out the door, overhearing his date ask, "What's a tiny mushroom?"

As soon as I am outside in the parking lot, I spot Carlow pacing near my car.

"Hey!"

Carlow grabs the sides of his waist tight, bends forward, and pushes out some quick breaths. I reach him and gently touch his shoulder.

"Hey you. I'm right here."

He stands up and faces me.

"Gah. That guy was right. I am a dweeb. You can do better than me."

"Seriously, Carlow? That was my toxic ex. He was terrible to me. He would not know a good, quality man if one ran over him with his Jeep."

"Quality?"

Carlow laughs derisively.

"Come here."

I pull him into my arms.

"I am in love with you. I love your quirkiness. I love being quirky with you. I love every moment I spend with you and want to spend endless moments with you. You're my person."

Carlow looks down at me, the anxiety leaving his eyes.

"Come home with me, Carlow. Let me show you how much I love you and how much I want to be with you."

I lead Carlow to my bedroom, kissing him the entire way. At the foot of my bed, I unbutton his red plaid shirt and pull him close to me while sitting down on the edge. I feel his arousal against my body and pull him on top of me once his shirt hits the floor.

We hungrily kiss, grinding into each other. He smells of pine and coffee. I place his hand on my breast, which is another first, and hear his breath catch.

"You feel so damn amazing, Fern. So soft."

"Want to lick them?"

I wiggle out of my t-shirt and quickly release my bra.

I don't even know how to describe Carlow's reaction to seeing my naked tits for the first time. His eyes widen, his mouth drops open, and he cups both of them.

"Go ahead. Taste them."

Carlow practically feeds off my nipples. His excitement is rough and I am in heaven. I show him how to lightly pinch my nipples and, when he does, a loud moan escapes my mouth. I feel his cock pulse at the sounds of my pleasure. I push my hips up into him, rubbing his thickness through his jeans.

"Holy," he huskily breathes out.

"Praying, are we? I have something that will make you see god."

I slip out of the rest of my clothes and work him out of his pants. And then, like the dork I am, did a small cheer.

Carlow laughs.

"What?"

"That, sir, is the most beautiful cock I have ever had the pleasure of meeting. Come here."

I help him to his back and straddle him. Taking his shaft, I wet the head with my swollen pussy. I love the way he is breathing. It is clear he is trying not to come on me right this very moment.

"Breathe, my love. I want to ride you."

With that said, I help him enter me as deeply as possible. We both groan in pleasure together. I reach out and pin his arms above his head, bouncing my large, heavy breasts in his face as I moan over and over. I am already so close and I can read his face that he's in the same predicament.

Our climaxes crash into each other, with us both grabbing at the other one, moaning, grunting, declaring our love for one another. We untangle in a sweaty mess, right as I notice rain falling outside the window.

We lie there naked, our limbs wrapped around each other, watching the raindrops decorate the window panes. He nuzzles his face into my neck.

"I'm glad I don't have to, but I could have easily waited 40 more years to experience that with you. It was well worth the wait."

8

CARLOW

The week before Halloween, we wake up to my cell ringing.

"Beck?" I asked, groggily.

"Dulce had the baby! A girl! Ten fingers, ten toes. I'm pretty sure a future mermaid tail. Visiting hours are at 9. Bring Fern!"

Fernanda and I arrive at the birthing center at the start of visiting hours, but the entire family is already there. Murphy and Mair, with their twins, Irvina and Marna, Lachlan and Paige, and Beck, strutting around like a proud peacock. Plus, my Aunt Luann and all 5 of her children and their wives. Plus Uncle Mitt and his husband Kent.

We take turns visiting Dulce in her room. When it is Fern's and my turn to meet baby Georgia, I am already overstimulated by the constant family cacophony. But when Beck places my niece in my arms, the tension and stress ease away.

"You look good like that," Fern whispers in my ear.

"I bet we would make good looking babies."

I feel a rush of embarrassment as my cheeks heat. I cannot believe I just said that out loud, in front of Beck and Dulce, even. But Fern's expression is not one of horror, but of sheer bliss.

"I think you're right. Maybe we can practice later," she seductively hisses into my ear.

Outside, in the waiting room, the din continues. Fern grabs my hand and squeezes it.

"Want to split? We can go home and just be."

This woman gets me like no other person in the world.

Epilogue

Fernanda

Wearing our wedding garb, we stand holding hands on the snow-covered beach. I turn to Carlow and tell him I am ready.

He lightly holds the sides of my head and kisses me like he has never kissed me before. I feel incredibly light and airy.

Carlow breaks the kiss and asks, "Ready?"

"Ready."

We dive into the ocean waves, holding hands, and together we swim deep into the depths. I do not feel the need to breathe because of the merman kiss he just gifted me. I do not feel chilled or bogged down. I feel one with the sea.

We reach an ocean cave and glide in. Murphy's father-in-law, the King of the Merpeople, is waiting for us, along with Carlow's brothers and their wives. Liora and my book club friends are also there, wearing diving suits. A rainbow of aquatic plants decorates the small cave, some giving off a glow.

We stop in front of the king, who is our officiant for the wedding ceremony. We wanted it small, short, and sweet. King Armund delivers.

Back on the beach, Carlow's brothers surprise us with a limousine to the airport. My hermit husband has never left California before, so we decided Maui is a perfect place to honeymoon. His brothers send us off in style.

In the back seat, we snuggle and look out at the snowy landscape.

"I can't wait to be inside of you in warm Hawaii," he whispers to me.

I slide my hand up his thigh.

"Me too, hubby, me too."

A MOUNTAIN
MERMAN
ROMANCE

THE MOUNTAIN MERMAN'S *Second Chance*

KAT VROMAN

1

MAIR

Ten Years past...

I basked in my freedom on Ravenhart Mountain. No royal duties. No delegations to greet. No sea-king father breathing down my neck about marriage.

If my mother had not advocated for me, my father never would have allowed me these four years to earn a degree. King Armund was adamant about setting me up for a royal intermarriage when I turned 18, but I refused. I want to be more than someone's queen. I want to do good in this world.

I demand to do good in this world.

Once we whittled down Daddy's reserves, he finally agreed to one school only - Ravenhart Mountain College, nestled in the mountains near our sea kingdom.

Fine. I would make it work.

And make it work I did.

I refused to be told by my daddy who I was going to be or who I was going to marry. I owned college. I owned my classes. I owned my grades. I owned the parties. I owned the pep rallies. I owned the late night studying.

I owned all aspects of my life during those college years, except for one part. I did not own my heart.

Professor Atwater, my Economic Sociology professor, owned every piece of my heart - and refused to accept it.

I am not an idiot. I know when a man wants me. And that man wanted me. Badly. He wanted my body, for sure, but Professor Atwater wanted my mind as well. We would get into these long, philosophical conversations after class or when I'd bump into him at the college library. I felt him soak me up during these interactions. I wanted to soak him up as well, but in bed.

He refused. Something about the professor/student relationship.

I left Ravenhart Mountain College with a Sociology degree and everything I set out to achieve in my college career. Well, minus Professor Atwater. I knew we had a connection, but he refused to cross that boundary.

Fine, his loss.

I'm taking on the world now.

Ten Years Later...

"Daddy, I'm working. I can't just stop in the middle of the day to go have lunch with some prince you scrounge up from Brisbane."

I stand outside my alma mater on a brisk October day. My assistant busies herself next to me while I partake in the never-ending argument with my father regarding some random prince he's dusted off for me.

"No, Daddy, I know that marriage is in my future. But, as I keep telling you, it will be on my terms. Hell, it may not even be with a prince."

I remove the phone from my ear as my father's temper bursts. I can't tell if he's angrier about the prince comment or the fact that I said hell. As his voice levels off, I continue speaking.

"Listen, I need to take a tour of my old school. I am a boatload of money to them, but I need to take a tour first to make sure it's a wise investment."

I say goodbye to my fuming father, gesture to my assistant Tina, and walk onto my old campus.

My alma mater is just as beautiful as it was a decade ago. Nestled in the foothills on the Corvid Valley side of Ravenhart Mountain, the campus is aglow with the reds, yellows, and oranges of autumn. I have not returned here since my graduation and am filled with conflicted emotion. I loved my time as a student, but this is also where my heart broke for the first, and last, time.

Buck up, buttercup. Onward and upward.

2

MURPHY

Ten Years Past...

My door slams shut.

The 21-year-old freakin' princess I am in love with just stormed out of my office and out of my life.

I looked out my window and saw her royal entourage swarm around her, like the queen bee she is. Mair apparently sensed me because she spun on her heels, flipping off my office window.

Sigh.

That young woman is a force. A spoiled, demanding, bratty force. A passionate, witty, bold, fiery, beautiful force. And, if I was younger and in a different profession, I would have already pledged my lifelong love and commitment to her.

31-year-old me is not younger. I am a 31-year-old assistant professor. Despite my broken heart, I have to adhere to both my professional and personal ethics.

Ten Years Later...

"Professor, the rep for the Luminary Depths Foundation will be here shortly," my secretary announces on the intercom.

"Thank you, Barb."

I clear off my desk so that I make a good impression. Whoever the foundation sent is the last person to have the say on whether the college earns their charitable grant. The dean decided I am the best person to lead them on the campus tour because, as she said, I ooze discipline and responsibility. She believes this will impress the foundation's rep.

I am positive it will just convince the rep that I am a stuffy bore, but hopefully I can show them how deserving our school and students are of this hefty grant.

I am just grateful that the foundation is sending a rep and not Mair. It's been around ten years since she stormed out of my life. I have kept up with her philanthropy via news reports and magazine spreads. I'm sure she is too busy for tour reviews like this one, but it is still a relief to hear the word rep.

Now, an associate professor, I have my eye on being promoted to a full professorship before I turn 45. For the past fifteen years, I have devoted myself to this school and its students. I have come to terms with the fact that I am to live a solo life. I have dated, but have never fallen hard for any of those women.

That happened once in my life, with the wrong person at the wrong time, and never again.

Do I sometimes wish I wasn't such an ethical killjoy? Yup. But I know I would make the same decision again. It was the right thing to do.

Sigh.

The intercom buzzes.

"Professor, Luminary Depths Foundation has arrived for their appointment."

I stand up, buttoning my suit jacket, and smoothing my tie. I

Kat Vroman

look up to find a familiar set of aquamarine eyes staring back at me. Underneath them, a very kissable mouth is agape.

3

Mair

I stand in my former professor's office doing my best goldfish impression.

I don't know who I was expecting, but I certainly was not expecting Professor Atwater.

"Where's the dean?" I ask, my voice so icy it could cut glass.

"Dean Price is currently out of the country. She requested I give the foundation its tour."

"Ah."

Now what?

"Uh, Ms. Delmar, we can start the tour when you are ready."

I stare at this man who curled my toes at age 21 and I fight the toe curl urge again. How is it even possible that Professor Atwater has grown even better looking with age? He continues to tower over my 5' 10" frame by a half foot, but he appears to have added even more muscle onto his human form. His dark blond hair and beard are graying in that perfect devour the professor way. Murphy's green eyes continue to look like emeralds, but I can see laugh lines framing them now.

"Of course," I reply as professionally as possible. "Lead the way."

Murphy takes me to various labs, classrooms, and facilities. He remains professional, and distant, which starts getting on my nerves about 30 minutes in. I feel antsy and ready to snap, so I channel that into a minor project.

A project to get under his skin. To get a rise out of him.

To make him blush like I did a decade ago.

"Ms. Delmar, the last part of the tour will be the animal husbandry area. First the stables."

"Stables? Sounds like a great place to interrupt two coeds," I say, airily, "Hell, it's the 21st century, maybe 3 coeds."

My assistant shoots me a look from her phone, but my eyes are on Murphy.

And he does not disappoint. His eyes widen as he quickly looks away from me. I see his cheeks flush underneath his beard. He clears his throat.

"I think we'll be safe from that, Ms. Delmar."

In the stables, I take my time greeting each horse while I think of how else to entertain myself.

"Sugar Cube here is pregnant and due within weeks," Murphy says as he leads me to a very pregnant painted horse.

"How exciting," I purr. "How about you, Professor Atwater? You must have a brood of kidlets now."

"I would love to be a father but, no, I do not have any children."

"Oh, well, I am sure you and your wife will be blessed soon."

"I will need to first find that wife," Murphy responds in a quiet voice.

I look up at him, not realizing how close he is standing to me next to Sugar Cube's stall. My breath catches when our eyes meet.

"I didn't realize," is all I could muster.

Murphy heads toward the exit, saying something about a vegetable garden. I follow, my body filling with a familiar desire. I am no longer antsy, but the warm, wet heat in my panties is demanding attention.

We end the tour in front of his office building.

"Thank you for the visit, Ms. Delmar. Please let me know if you have any further questions and I hope this is the start of a long relationship between the college and the foundation."

"Thank you, professor," I say as I catch his cheeks turning slightly pink. "I will be dining at Mountain Peak Steakhouse tonight. Alone. I would love some company. We can catch up?"

Murphy's eyes meet mine in surprise, but I can see a heat there that I have not witnessed in ten years.

"I can make that work."

"Great, I'll see you there at 7."

I enter the restaurant's foyer to find Murphy waiting for me. He has changed into dark jeans and a button-up shirt that is snug enough to show off the curves of his muscles.

I watch him take in the sight of me. I am wearing an eggplant colored dress with a scoop neck, accentuating my ample chest. Sparks dance around my clit when I notice his eyes linger on my cleavage.

"Shall we?" I ask, brushing past him. He smells like parchment and coffee.

At dinner, we catch up. I talk about my foundation work, how my father would rather I be on my fourth kid by now, and my plans for the future. He talks about the college and his brothers. The meal comes and goes, but we continue chatting, reaching the level of ease we had with each other ten years ago. Our server walks up with a dessert menu.

"Ma'am, sir, many of our guests enjoy coffee and dessert on our back patio to watch the fireflies this time of year. Would you like to be escorted out there?"

Murphy eyes me.

"I would love that. Professor?"

"Yes, that sounds great, although you need to call me Murphy."

I want to devour his sexy smile and crinkly eyes in one bite.

"Alright, but that means you have to call me Mair, Prof...Murphy."

"Fair enough."

On the patio, we are the only couple, minus one canoodling in a dark corner. The waiter was right. The fireflies are putting on a show for us. Murphy follows me as I walk to the railing. I sense him standing close behind, his body heat warming the side of my shoulder and neck. I turn toward him.

Our eyes meet, and he steps closer to me.

4

Murphy

All day I have wanted to grab Mair and claim her as mine, but I held back. After a couple of glasses of merlot, my will power shatters.

She stares up at me as I cup her chin.

"May I kiss you?" I barely breathe out the words.

"Yes."

Mair threads her fingers into my belt buckles and pulls herself onto her tiptoes.

The first kiss I have dreamt of for over ten years does not start like I imagined. Instead of soft and sweet, we are roughly, hungrily pressing our lips together, mouths open, tongues searching. She tastes like red wine and peppercorn. I feel her heart pounding through her breasts, which are pressed up against my chest. We are both gripping each other close, although I allow my hands to roam. I grab her large, round ass, and she gives a little moan. I'm fully erect now and Mair lets me know she's aware by grinding onto me.

"Ahem," the waiter interrupts us with our coffees.

"Thank you." Mair takes her cup and sits down.

I watch her take a sip. Her shiny strawberry blond hair is a mess now. It makes her look even younger.

Gah, what am I even doing? Mair may not be my student anymore, but I am an old fart next to her. Dammit, I'm an idiot for agreeing to have dinner with her.

"Uh, Mair, I need to go. I'm sorry. This wasn't right of me."

I grab my jacket and take off, feeling her hurt stare following me.

The next morning at work, I am a distracted mess. I think I made the right call last night, but I ache for her.

My intercom buzzes.

"Sir, just a reminder that you have a lunch appointment with Drayce Serpico at noon at Mountain Peak Steakhouse."

I smack my forehead a little too hard. I forgot about my lunch with my friend and I forgot it is at the same place where I ate last night. Time to get my head back into the game.

I arrive early and grab us a table where I don't have to look at the patio or where I sat with Mair the previous evening. Drayce walks in, getting a few stares from folks who I assume are tourists on the mountain. Drayce's lizardfolk clan have made Ravenhart Mountain their home since before I was born, but they typically keep to themselves. My friend has always been a little different from his clansmen, even working with me at the college for a few years.

"I see no shirt, no shoes, no service still does not apply to you," I joke as he sits down.

"The men here should be grateful I am wearing pants or their women would already be at my side," Drayce responds, dryly

"How are you, friend? It's been a few months."

We catch up over lunch. He's very focused on finding a partner for himself. Lizardfolk are always male and must look outside their own kind to find a mate. This causes issues given their distinct look and, along with only male babies born as lizardfolk, keeps their clan numbers small.

"What about you, Murphy? You're getting up there in years. Are you ready to settle down yet?"

I stretch in my seat and shake my head.

"Lord, you don't even know. And, hey, I've always been willing to settle down. I just have never met someone appropriate to settle down with."

"Well, besides that student. What was her name? Maria?"

"Mair. And she was not appropriate in the slightest. Like you said, she was my student."

Drayce gives me a wry smile. I give up, sigh, and continue.

"I just saw Mair yesterday."

"What?"

Though Drayce's lizard features typically mute his facial expressions, surprise clearly shows on his face.

"Yeah, she runs a foundation and they may give the college a large grant. I gave her a tour yesterday."

"How did that go?"

"We ended up making out at dinner."

Drayce bellows out a laugh, clapping his hands together.

"Well, it's about time!"

"Are you kidding? I know she's not my student anymore, but she's a decade younger than I am. I ended up stopping it and bailing. I feel like an asshole, but it had to be done."

Drayce shakes his head.

"Murph, for a smart man, you can be such a fucking dolt.

There has been no one else since Mair. No one at least that you have kept around for more than a few months. You don't see this woman for like ten years and in less than 24 hours you two are locking lips? Bro, she's your mate."

I don't respond, but I do order a whiskey. Did I mess this up? Am I overthinking?

Hell, maybe it was just a kiss for Mair, anyway. She is used to getting whatever she wants.

After work, I pop by the market to buy ingredients for my favorite chicken dinner. When I arrive home to my cabin on Lake Summit, I find Mair sitting on my deck steps. I open my mouth to greet her, but she stops me in my tracks with an angry tirade.

"Listen, Professor Murphy Atwater, I am done with you clinging to ethics that matter no more. I am a grown ass woman. You are a grown ass man. I have not been your student since my early 20s. Yesterday proved to me that I am in love with you. And you are in love with me, dammit. So get off your Amish bullshit and get over yourself!"

I stand there, blinking like a moron, holding my grocery bag, and staring at her fiery blue eyes.

Mair is the most incredible woman I have ever known and will ever know. I understand that now. I am a fool.

"Want chicken parmesan and caesar salad for dinner?"

5

Mair

"I've thought about you a lot through the years," I admit to Murphy as we eat the meal he cooked.

"Yeah, same."

My heart swells. I have longed to hear this man tell me he is into me. Ten years ago it was long, intense looks but rejection with words.

Dinner is less formal and more relaxed than last night. We laugh more. He lets me touch his hand without pulling away. He tells me I'm beautiful.

"I have never been more attracted to a man than I am to you. Not once."

Murphy laughs.

"Seriously? Even with this old man gray?"

"I like it."

I stand up and walk to his side of the table. I straddle his lap, facing him, and stroke his graying beard. Murphy looks at me with his cool green eyes and I fall right onto his lips.

Kissing him yesterday had been frantic and desperate. Today, though, it is soft and intimate. His beard is rough against my skin.

Then it is rough against my neck. Then against my clavicle. I decide to go for it and pull my shirt over my head.

"Fuck," Murphy grunts out, diving his face in between my cleavage, his hands already on the clasps.

Within seconds, my bra is thrown across the kitchen and the man of my dreams is licking my tits. Murphy pauses his tongue exploration once in a while to look at my breasts and bounce them with his hands.

"Absolutely fucking perfect. I knew they would be."

I grind on his lap while he enjoys my nipples some more. Then Murphy stands up abruptly, lifting me with his arms under my ass, and carries me into his bedroom. He tosses me on the bed, like I'm a rag doll, and starts working my pants off. Before I have time to demand that he take off some clothes, too, his face is in between my thighs. It takes mere minutes for his tongue flicking and sucking on my clit before my orgasm crashes like a wave down my entire naked body.

I catch my breath and demand, "Clothes. Off. Now. I need you in me."

Murphy follows my demands by dropping his pants to the ground. When he releases his cock from his briefs, I gasp. I have never been with a man with such a large cock before. My pussy is throbbing and I play with it with one hand. The other hand beckons him to me.

"I want you inside of me."

His shirt now on the floor, Murphy crawls over to me on the bed. He strokes the head of his cock while kissing my neck and then slides his thickness into me.

"Fuck, yes, you're so tight. I knew you would be," he whispers in my ear.

I wrap my legs around his hips as he pounds away inside of me. We kiss and whisper, "I love yous" from time to time. Our moaning becomes in sync and we come at the same time.

Soon after, I fall asleep in his arms.

6

Murphy

Mair and I spent every waking second together during the weekend. Back in my office on Monday, I feel a mixture of elation and impatience because I want to be with her.

My cell beeps and it's a text from Mair saying the foundation's board approved the grant for the college. Her assistant will call Barb to set up a meeting to review everything and that she will see me tonight for dinner.

I drive down to Branwen Beach after work so that Mair doesn't have to schlep up the mountain again. We meet at Mare Pacificum, a restaurant situated right on the beach. We dine on mussels, clams, and shrimp. After dinner, we take a long walk along the beach.

"So, do you have something to wear to the gala this weekend, my sexy date?"

"I do. I hope it's not too drab for the princess's arm candy."

Mair giggles, then gasps, like she just remembered something.

"I almost forgot. My father may attend tomorrow's meeting."

"I am having an audience with the sea king?"

Mair's reaction to my question meant I did not say that as chill as I meant to.

"You'll be fine, Murph. He is all bark, no bite. And this is my foundation. I think he's just being extra supportive since we're giving the grant to my alma mater."

I must still look worried because she grabs my hand and yanks me toward the water.

"I have to get going. Be a gentleman and take me to the entrance of the kingdom?"

I kiss her, and we shed our clothing. Mair, seductively naked, places her clothes inside her handbag. We walk, hand in hand, into the water. She transitions into her mermaid form, something I have never seen her do. Her tail, covered in iridescent shades of silver, blue, and pink, shimmers under the ocean. Her large breasts are floating, with her tan nipples beckoning to me. I kiss her under the waves and transform as well.

We stare at each other in our pure forms. I have seen no one look as radiant as she does. We both laugh, bubbles trailing above us to the surface. The genuine joy I feel right now will be almost impossible to match again.

Once at the entrance to the merpeople kingdom, we embrace one more time, our slippery forms twisting around each other as we kiss deeply. We float there, twisted like a glazed cruller, holding each other tightly. I wrap my arms around her neck.

"You were made for me, Mair Delmar."

"I know," she whispers back.

The meeting with the foundation is scheduled right before

the end of the day. I am once again a ball of nerves and decide to walk around the campus before the meeting. When that doesn't help, I opt to wait in the conference room and goof off on my phone to relax.

As I walk down the hall to the college's large meeting room, I hear angry voices behind the partially open door.

"No daughter of mine is going to be in love with an instructor!"

"He is an associate professor, Daddy, and you don't get to decide who I may or may not fall in love with."

"You have a responsibility, as princess, to our kingdom, Mair. I have humored your whims long enough."

"Whims? Luminary Depths Foundation is not a whim, Father," Mair's voice drips with indignation, "I have worked my ass off building it and donating to causes I believe will help our world."

"That very well may be so, but you are the princess of the Sea-Maid Kingdom. You must marry a suitable man."

They continue to argue as I stand outside, not sure what to do with myself. I love Mair but she also deserves the absolute best. The absolute best includes a peaceful family life. Not drama and screaming matches. Not a basic college professor when she could have someone dashing, worldly, and wealthy.

I cannot allow her to throw everything away because of me.

I throw open the door, interrupting their quarrel.

"Mair, I think your father is right."

King Armund lifts his chin proudly while Mair spits out, "Excuse me?"

"Your father only wants the best for you. I cannot, in good conscience, be an obstacle in your life's path or your happiness."

"Fantastic. That's settled," the king says smugly.

"The hell it is!"

Mair stands in the middle of us, looking back and forth between our faces, fists clenched by her side.

7

Mair

"The two of you appear to be under the impression that I am to be told what to do and how to live my life," my words come out with a slow force.

"Daughter, we..."

"Excuse me, I am speaking."

My father looks taken aback.

"As I was saying, I am a grown ass adult woman. I'm fricken 31-years-old. I decide who I am in love with. I decide the path my life takes. I do not need two men telling me how to live my friggin life."

Tears are burning my eyes, which makes me angrier. I turn to my father.

"Daddy, I need you to move on from this. I can't keep justifying my life choices to you. I refuse to do so any longer."

The tears are now falling down my cheeks as I turn to Murphy.

"I expected more from you. I thought you found the adult in me instead of viewing me forever as your silly student."

I hear Murphy attempt to respond, but I bolt out of the

room, picking up speed in the hallway, and I am running by the time I hit the steps outside.

I stand in the dress shop in my gown for the gala as Lara, the seamstress, makes her finishing touches. My friend, Artina, waits her turn while listening to me vent.

"I am so tired of being treated like a child by the men in my life."

"I still can't believe you've finally hooked up with Professor Atwater," Artina says dreamily. "He was my favorite teacher at school."

"Arti, it's not even a hookup. I am head over heels for this man. And I know he feels the same about me. Which makes me even more pissed that he tried to break it off because of my fricken father."

"Head over heels? Really? That's so romantic," Artina pretends to swoon.

I laugh. I love this girl.

"Enough about my crap. How's it going with that new guy?"

"Meh, I'm over it. I don't think I am meant to date a fellow bear shifter. We're so growly."

Lara finishes my dress and instructs me to take it off in the dressing room. Once Artina is done, we thank her as she tells us that the dresses will be ready first thing in the morning.

As we walk to our cars, Artina stops me in the parking lot.

"Hey, if you really love him and think he feels the same, then cut him some slack. I doubt it's easy falling for the freaking sea king's only daughter."

She has a point.

Murphy and I texted a bit after the big blowup, but he respected my request for some space. I told him I would meet him at the gala because I'm not ready to be alone with him yet. I enter the ballroom and find him chatting with my father. They are both smiling and laughing.

Did I enter a different dimension when I walked through the doors?

"Dad? Murphy?"

"There you are," my father responds cheerfully.

Murphy turns to me, smiling but with a seriousness in his green eyes.

"Hey you. Please, I have to apologize. I had no right to try to dictate what choices are right for you. I feel like an ass."

"So do I, Daughter. I know this has been an issue between us for some time, but you are right. You're 31. You're an adult."

"A grown ass adult," I respond with pride, making my father laugh.

"Exactly," my mother says as she walks up, giving me a peck on the cheek, then grabbing my father's hand and leading him to the dance floor.

"Care to join them?" Murphy bows, offering me his hand.

I curtsy and take it. The heat from his touch warms my

panties. We dance as close as possible on the floor, staring deep into each other's eyes. He places a kiss between my eyes and puts our foreheads together.

"Us together makes sense. You're a smart, smart woman, Mair Delmar."

8

MURPHY

"Happy one-year anniversary, beautiful."

I hand Mair a mixed autumn bouquet.

"These are gorgeous. I can't believe it's been an entire year already."

"I can't believe we've lived together for over two months now."

"Well, I can't believe we are about to break ground on a new mountain school together."

I pull her close to me.

"That's because of you, babe. You and your foundation. Without your support, it wouldn't have been possible."

Mair lightly kisses me and nuzzles into my neck.

"It's because of you that this idea even came to be. A school for orphaned shapeshifter children is much needed in this country. And I could not think of a better dean for the school than Professor Atwater."

"I guess we are both amazing."

Mair giggles and sticks her tongue out at me, so I steal it with my mouth. Soon my hands are up her shirt and she is pulling down my sweats.

"Do we have time?" I breathe into her ear as I slide my hand down her skirt and panties, inserting two fingers into her hot, wet pussy.

I fingerfuck her while rubbing my thumb on her clit. She loses her mind when I kiss her neck and trace it with my tongue.

"Get your ass on the couch," Mair manages to force out during moans.

I obey and am rewarded with her riding me reverse cowboy while she plays with her clit. Mair's round ass looks amazing as she bounces on my shaft. I grab her hips and roughly help her pound onto me.

"Fuck, Professor Atwater, your cock feels so good in my tight pussy."

That's all it took. I explode into her as she yells curses while coming.

Two hours later, we stand at the site of our future school. Autumn leaves surround us in the trees and we stare out onto Corvid Valley below. Farmland, ranches, and more fall colors.

Mair and I hold each other in the crisp air. She smiles up at me in her cute beanie with a rosy red nose from the cold. I give it a kiss.

"I smell rain," she says.

"Same. We should head back, but there's just one thing I need to do."

Mair looks at me with a confused expression, but her eyes change to elation when she watches me fall to one knee.

I take the ring box out of my coat pocket and flip it open.

"Mair Anna Delmar, everyday I think about how grateful I am that you came back into my life. You have brought so much to my little world. Passion. Persistence. Direction. Fun. Mind blowing sex. Adventure. Purpose. You complete me. I never want to leave your side. Will you marry me, Mair Delmar?"

Next thing I know, I am flat on my back in the fallen leaves with my future wife covering me in kisses shouting "Yes! Yes! Yes!"

Epilogue

MAIR

A royal wedding is an affair for the century, or so my mother claims.

My father had a stadium with oxygen-filled box seats built just for the event so that our land-loving friends and allies can comfortably attend. And attend, they do. I stand before the entrance with the bridal runner under my feet, my sea king father by my side, and I peer out at the massive audience. Ocean lilies and coral adorn the entire stadium. Gorgeous gowns and sparkly jewels are everywhere I look. My insanely handsome fiance stands at the front, his 3 brothers standing beside him, and my bridesmaids walk into position.

"It is time, my amazing daughter."

"I love you, Daddy."

My father gives my arm a squeeze, and we begin the procession down the aisle.

The sea priest greets us and asks, "Who gives this woman to be married to this man?"

My father clears his throat and booms out, "She gives herself to this man, Father."

Artina, stunning in her bridesmaid dress, catches my eye and mouths, "Nice."

Our ceremony is full of pomp and circumstance. The reception includes so many courses that I lose track. Our wedding cake, shaped like the college we met in, is full of fresh fruit to celebrate summer. Pop star Piper Falk, to the absolute joy of my younger cousins, sings for our first dance.

We end the night with the stadium rising to the ocean surface to view a spectacular drone show. Murphy stands behind me, holding me tight as we watch the colorful configurations.

"I love you, my wife," he whispered in my ear.

I turn my head and meet his eyes.

"I am pregnant, my husband."

Murphy spins me around and lifts me straight into the air. Our lips lock together as he brings me back down. We are on the adventure of our life.

Stalk Me!

Instagram
Facebook
Website

Free Novelette!

Join Kat Vroman's author newsletter to stay updated on paranormal quickies and new releases, plus get *The Mountain Horseman's Flame* novelette for free! Scan the QR code below:

About the Author

A Masshole Californian in the streets and a paranormal romance writer in the sheets, Kat Vroman pens steamy novelettes for the busy reader who doesn't have time to wait for a Happily Ever After. A full-time working single mom herself, she understands the need to steal an hour or two for a magical escape from the everyday grind.

Kat's paranormal quickies feature Gen X and Elder Millennial protagonists, because true love can strike us at any age. And a graying mountain merman can be damn sexy, right?!

Off the page, Kat's world centers around juggling her day job, a hilarious tween, fur babies, parenting a college kid, and practicing the art of being a joyful feminist killjoy. Through her writing and her life, Kat demonstrates that even in the busiest of days, there's always room for a little magic.

www.ingramcontent.com/pod-product-compliance
Ingram Content Group UK Ltd.
Pitfield, Milton Keynes, MK11 3LW, UK
UKHW041936030225
454602UK00004B/381